The book: Intro

In the deep forests of Jotunheim, where the morning mist hangs like a veil between the trees and time seems to stand still, a world of magic and mystique unfolds. Here, in this realm of wild landscapes and unpredictable forces, our story begins.

This is the story of Skrymir, a young giant whose fate is closely intertwined with the ancient gods and the mighty giants. Jotunheim is a world reminiscent of the Nordic lands, but its forests are filled with more than just trees and wildlife. They are home to gods, giants, and other magical beings, where order and chaos battle for dominance.

It is here, in this tumultuous land, that Skrymir discovers a fateful event that will change his life forever. A destiny tied to a small wolf cub named Fenris, whose innocent appearance hides a powerful and decisive role in Norse mythology.

Thus begins the journey for our hero, a journey through dangerous forests, treachery, and heroic deeds. A journey that will test his courage, his will, and his relationship with the forces that govern the universe.

Welcome to Jotunheim, where Skrymir's fate unfolds in the shadows of the ancient gods' struggle for power and survival.

Chapter 1: The Forests of Jotunheim

In the deep forests of Jotunheim, where massive trees tower overhead and block out much of the sky, there's a place of stunning beauty and mystery. This forest, with its mist weaving through the treetops and patches of sunlight brightening the ground, is wild and untamed.

It's a quiet place, yet it feels alive with countless whispers and the smell of old secrets carried on the breeze. Clear rivers flow and mountains stand tall like ancient protectors. This is where dreams and adventures come to life.

In these woods, you'll find everything from stunning Vættir to terrifying monsters. It's a place of beauty and danger, where life thrives in every corner.

The huge trees, covered in moss and ferns, reach toward the sky, looking ancient and wise. Their branches stretch upwards, and their leaves rustle in the wind, whispering secrets of old.

Under these giant trees, a mix of wildflowers and herbs blankets the ground, adding splashes of color to the moist soil. Light and shadow play between the tree trunks, creating a mesmerizing dance, while the constant buzz of insects celebrates the forest's vibrant life.

Here in the deep forests of Jotunheim wanders Skrymir, his steps light and cautious on the soft forest floor. Around him, the trees rise like mighty watchtowers, stretching towards the sky with their branches forming a dense roof over his head. These trees, ancient and wise, bear stories from the dawn of time and secrets that are only revealed to those worthy of listening..

As he walks, Skrymir lets his hand glide over the rough bark of the trees, as if trying to read their history in the deep scratches and cracks. His eyes continuously search for signs of life in the dark heart of the forest, while he is driven by an inner urge to explore and discover.

But even though the forest's beauty is captivating, there is also a sense of unease lurking in the shadows. Behind each tree and under every stone, an unknown danger may hide, and even the most innocent sounds might turn out to be warnings of dangers lurking in the dark forest.

Yet, Skrymir continues his journey, his courage unshakable and his curiosity unquenchable. He knows that secrets and adventures await beyond each bend in the path, and he is determined to explore them all, regardless of the dangers that may await.

Skrymir stopped in the middle of the path and let his gaze slowly sweep over the enchanting forest that spread around him. His heart beat faster with excitement, and his eyes shone with budding anticipation as he absorbed the beauty and mysteries of the forest.

He let his hand stroke the rough bark of a nearby tree, feeling its ancient wisdom sink into his soul. The tree's strength and calm gave him a sense of security amidst the unknown, and he knew he was on the right path toward something great and significant.

As he moved through the dim interior of the forest, he was surrounded by sounds of life and magic. He heard the birds' song, casting their tones into the air like pearls on a string, and he sensed the forest's hidden inhabitants moving silently through the underbrush and shadows.

Each time he reached a clearing or an opening in the treetops, new vistas and opportunities for adventure opened up. He could feel the budding anticipation of what lay ahead, like a buzzing electricity in the air, filling him with an irrepressible desire to explore and discover.

Skrymir knew that the forest was filled with secrets and mysteries waiting to be unveiled, and he was determined to follow his dreams and seek the truth, regardless of the dangers that might await on the other side of the dense walls of trees.

Thus, Skrymir continued his journey through the beauty and mysteries of the forest, ready to embrace the unknown and discover his destiny in the enchanting lands of Jotunheim. He arrived at an opening in the forest, where he could hear water—it must be Elivågen, he thought to himself.

Skrymir wandered along the rushing banks of Elivågen, his mind filled with curiosity and anticipation. His steps led him to a secluded part of the river, where he suddenly discovered a small island in the middle of the stream. On the island sat a lonely wolf cub, whose eyes reflected deep sadness and longing.

Skrymir stood facing the island, with the wolf's lonely figure as his only company in the midst of Elivågen's rushing stream. Elivågen, the river that cuts through Jotunheim, is a mighty waterway, whose currents rush with a force that seems to pull even the mountains together. Its waters are deep and untouched, and its surface glimmers like silver in the sunlight as it winds through the lush landscape.

Skrymir stood on the bank of Elivågen, observing its majestic flow. Despite his determination, he was hindered by the river's strength and violent currents, making any crossing impossible without the right equipment or the accompaniment of a powerful ally.

The longer he looked, the more he could see that the island was sinking. The powerful current in the river was eating away more and more of the island. He thought he must save the poor wolf cub.

A sudden movement caught his attention as a serpent came sliding forth from the bushes. Skrymir observed it with a mix of curiosity and caution. The serpent began to speak, with a voice filled with promises and secrets.

"In a cave, not far from here, is a spider guarding a special drink," said the serpent, turning its head towards a distant cliffside.

"This drink can enlarge me, so I can reach the wolf cub and free him from the island. If you are brave enough to accompany me into the cave and help me steal the spider's drink, I will be able to save the wolf cub from the rising water."

Skrymir turned his gaze towards the cliffside and felt doubt gnawing at him. But with a look at the wolf cub, whose eyes still reflected deep longing, he made a decision. "I'm ready, let's save the wolf cub," he said to the serpent and began following it to the cave.

As they reached the cave entrance, they were met by a claustrophobic darkness. Skrymir cut a torch from a nearby tree and lit it, illuminating the cave's interior with a faint glow. Together, they moved deeper into the darkness, filled with a creeping sense of unease.

Suddenly, they heard a sharp rustle overhead, and a cold shiver ran down Skrymir's spine as a giant spider crawled forth from the shadows. With its black eyes gleaming like coal, the spider stared threateningly at them, and its claws scraped against the cave floor in anticipation of a fight.

Skrymir gripped the torch tightly, ready for battle, while the serpent hissed its challenge to the spider. The two allies stood together against the fearsome opponent and threw themselves into a desperate fight to steal the spider's drink and save the wolf cub from its lonely fate on the sinking island.

The spider whirled around in the cave with a rattling sound, its claws snarled, and its jaws snapped threateningly together. Skrymir stood ready with his torch raised, prepared to meet the fearsome opponent. The serpent slithered smoothly around the spider, its body dancing in elegant curves in an attempt to distract it.

The fight was intense, a tangle of movements and sounds that filled the cave. Skrymir's torch flickered in the darkness, casting crooked shadows on the wet cave walls. He tried to keep the spider at bay with the flaming light of the torch, but the spider was quick and dodged his attempts with merciless ease. Each time Skrymir tried to get closer, he was met by the spider's sharp claws and poisonous bite.

The serpent wove around the spider like a cloud of smoke, its bite trying to reach its vulnerable spots, but the spider defended itself with impressive skill. The serpent hissed and hissed, its eyes glittering in the darkness, but it was clear that the fight was reaching its climax.

Skrymir realized that he had to act quickly. With a fearless roar, he lunged at the spider, his torch whirling in the air like a sword of fire, and he threw himself into the fight with all his strength and courage. He managed to land several precise blows, but the spider fought back with wild determination.

Suddenly, Skrymir saw his moment. With a quick movement, he dodged the spider's attack and struck it at the eyes. The spider let out a deafening scream and retreated, its body trembling with pain.

Skrymir took a deep breath, his chest heaving with effort, but his eyes gleamed with triumph. He turned to the serpent, which rested on the cave floor beside him. "We've done it," he said with a voice filled with relief and joy.

The serpent nodded silently, its eyes shining with an inner glow. "Yes, we have defeated the spider," it replied and turned its gaze towards the glistening vessel at the end of the cave.
With heaving chests and relieved minds, they stood facing each other, their gazes meeting in a quiet understanding of what they had just achieved.

"You are brave," said the serpent in a whisper that sounded like the wind rushing through the trees. "Your will and determination have brought us victory."

The serpent looked at Skrymir, "What is your name, brave giant?" "Skrymir," Skrymir replied.

"What is your name?" asked Skrymir. "Jormungandr," the serpent answered, "you can just call me Midgard, that's what everyone I know does."

"Why do they call you Midgard?" asked Skrymir. "Because when I was a little serpent , I wasn't very big." "So I was called Midgard, because in Midgard worms are not very big, and they thought I was a little worm," said Midgard with a slightly sad expression.

Skrymir nodded understandingly, not knowing what to say. "I myself am sometimes called Utgard-Loki, because I come from the same desolate region of Jotunheim." Midgard looked back in surprise. Skrymir then said, "It was a tough fight, but together we overcame the spider. Now we must continue and save the wolf cub from the sinking island."

Midgard nodded in agreement. "Yes, the wolf cub is waiting for our help." "Let's not wait any longer."

With their goal in mind, they left the cave and headed towards the riverbank, where the sinking island awaited them. The rushing streams of Elivagar stood between them and the wolf. Skrymir glanced at the mighty waters and sighed.

When they reached the shore, they could see the lone wolf cub sitting on the edge of the island, staring out over the rushing water.

Midgard told Skrymir to give him the magic potion from the spider's cave. Skrymir brought the magical drink to his mouth and he drank it. Instantly, a transformation occurred, and Midgard began to grow in size, his body becoming thicker and longer, his shiny scales stretching out to an impressive length. Now, in his enlarged form, he could reach the wolf cub on the island.

With a deep breath, the serpent bent down and gently lifted the wolf cub up with his massive body. The wolf cub looked surprised, but quickly a gratitude spread over his face as he realized they had come to save him.

The serpent, now in its impressively enlarged form, carried the wolf across the rushing waters of Elivagar and gently laid him down on the riverbank by Skrymir's side. The wolf looked in wonder at the large serpent now standing before him as a protector, and his eyes twinkled with gratitude.

"You... you are truly a friend," said the wolf in a gentle voice, his fur shimmering in the sunlight.

The serpent nodded with its mighty head. "We have come to help you." "No one should be alone in this world."

Skrymir smiled and stepped forward to greet the wolf. "Welcome back to the world, friend. What is your name?"

The wolf hesitated for a moment before answering: "I... I don't know. "I was always called Fenris by the one who brought me here."

"Fenris," repeated Skrymir with a nod. "A fitting name for such a majestic creature as you."

Fenris looked melancholically over the river, the memories of loneliness on the island stabbing at his heart like a dagger. "I never thought I would see anyone again," he said with a sniffle.

"Now you are no longer alone," said Skrymir comfortingly. "We are here for you."

Together, the three sat by the riverbank, sharing stories of their experiences and adventures. Fenris talked about the long days on the island, where he dreamed of returning to the outside world. Skrymir spoke of his travels through Jotunheim and the brave actions that had led him to the serpent and Fenris' rescue. And Midgard, with his wisdom and understanding of the world, listened and shared his own insights with both of them.

Fenris looked at his new friends with gratitude in his eyes. "Thank you for bringing me back to the world," he said.

The serpent smiled and nodded. "You seemed like a good friend, Fenris. And friends always help each other."

Fenris smiled and his tail wagged.

The day broke with a golden glow, casting its warm light over Jotunheim. Skrymir, Fenris, and Midgard stood together by the riverbank, while Midgard's tail had coiled itself into the surrounding bushes.

"It has been an eventful day," said Skrymir, turning to Fenris with a smile. "Even though we just met, I feel we have already experienced so much together."

Fenris nodded and looked down at the ground. "Yes, we have." "I didn't know what to expect when I woke up today."

Skrymir placed a reassuring hand on Fenris' shoulder. "None of us did, but here we are, both in the midst of an adventure in this wonderful world."

Fenris looked up with a wondering expression. "But my father has left me, and I have no one to return to."

Skrymir shook his head. "You are not alone, Fenris." "We can travel together, just us against the world." "I promise you, I will be there for you, no matter what happens."

A feeling of relief spread through Fenris, and he smiled gratefully. "Thank you, Skrymir. I will follow you, and we will create our own adventures together."

Midgard, who had drunk deeply of the magic potion, had now grown so large that one could not see the end of his tail when looking down his body. With the size now came an unexpected challenge. Midgard found himself trapped among the trees that surrounded the riverbank, unable to move freely on land.

"I fear I have become too big," said Midgard with a deep rumble in his voice, reminiscent of distant thunder. "I can no longer navigate through the forest without destroying everything in my path."

Skrymir and Fenris looked worriedly at their friend, who now threatened to cause chaos wherever he went.

"We need to do something," said Skrymir, looking seriously at Fenris. "Otherwise, we will all be caught by Midgard's relentless growth."

Fenris nodded in agreement and turned his gaze to the magnificent serpent. "What do you want us to do, Midgard?"

Midgard sighed heavily and looked down at the riverbank, where the water flowed quietly by. "I think I need to be rolled out into the river," he said with a certain sadness in his voice. "I can only move freely in the water now, and it seems that is my only home." "I've always hated water, but it's my only way out."

Skrymir and Fenris exchanged a look filled with understanding. They both knew it was the only option to save Midgard from a lifetime of isolation and limitation on land.

Together they went to Midgard, and with care, they pushed the great serpent into the river, where it disappeared beneath the surface with a deep splash. In the clear water, they could see Midgard glide freely, its scales glittering like diamonds under the sun.

The two turned away from the river and began to walk away from the river. They could feel a sense of relief and peace spreading in their hearts. They had perhaps said goodbye to a friend, but they had also done what was best for Midgard. And although they were now separated by the water, they knew their friendship would last forever, no matter what challenges the world brought them.

Meanwhile, Midgard swam through the river, still growing. He thought to himself, "probably shouldn't have drunk so much magic potion."

Then Midgard had an idea and found two bottles by the riverbank. With a little spit, he filled each with magical drink, two beautiful bottles with golden contents. One bottle was large, filled to the brim with the magic drink, while the other was smaller, only half full.

Midgard looked at the two bottles with a smile and thought of his friends. Fenris would love the power and strength that the magic drink would give him, while Skrymir, who could not handle as much as Fenris, would have to settle for a smaller dose.

With the bottles in his mouth and a sense of generosity in his heart, Midgard swam to Skrymir and Fenris, who were sitting by the bank of a small stream, resting in the shade. With a nimble movement, Midgard placed the bottles in front of them and looked expectantly at their reactions.

Fenris' eyes lit up when he saw the large bottle, "What is this?" he asked.

"It's magic potion, I think I've had enough," replied Midgard.
Fenris jumped up to take it in his jaws. "Thank you, Midgard! This will make me stronger!"

Skrymir smiled gratefully and carefully picked up the smaller bottle. "Thank you, friend. I'm sure this will help me on my adventures."

Fenris gulped down the bottle's contents. Skrymir looked on in astonishment. He took a small sip from the bottle and threw it away, "Yuck," he said loudly.

Midgard looked pleased as his friends thanked him, and with a feeling of joy and satisfaction in his heart, he returned to the river to begin his new journey through Jotunheim's deep waters.

Skrymir stared at Fenris with a mix of awe and wonder. He knew his life would never be the same again. Skrymir looked up at the sky. Something felt different, as if the universe was holding its breath in anticipation of something big and fateful.

"Fenris," said Skrymir with a voice that bore traces of a distant past and a peculiar wisdom. "I believe your destiny is connected to the forces that govern our world." "You are chosen to walk a path that will lead you through danger and fear, but also through courage and magic."

Fenris looked back, with a puzzled expression, as if someone else had carried Skrymir's voice. So he just nodded.

Chapter 2: The Meeting with Suttung

As dusk fell over the forests of Jotunheim, Fenris and Skrymir stood by the riverbank, having just bid farewell to their friend, Midgard. Shadows grew around them, and the sounds of the forest intensified as if preparing for the night.

"Fenris," said Skrymir, turning to the young wolf. "It's getting late, and we should head home for some food."

Fenris nodded, his dark eyes reflecting the forest's mysterious depths. "Yes, that's a good idea. I've become hungry after the long time on the island without food."

Together, they ventured into the dense foliage of the forest, where the branches of the trees created a dark canopy above them, dimming the light from the last rays of the sunset. The path was uneven under their feet, and the sounds of the forest's nightlife surrounded them with an atmosphere of excitement and mystery.

Along the way, they shared stories and memories from their adventures together, and their laughter echoed through the forest's silence, creating a bond between them stronger than any blood tie.

After a while, they broke through the trees and stepped into a clearing where Skrymir's home lay, a simple hut hidden among the trees. A bit of smoke still rose from the chimney, and there was a scent of homely warmth and cooking.

Skrymir opened the door and invited Fenris inside with a smile. "Welcome home," he said. "Let's eat and rest our tired feet. Tomorrow new adventures await."

Fenris, now a large wolf, sat by the fire in Skrymir's hut and stared into the flames with a distant expression in his yellow eyes. Skrymir, sensing a heaviness in the air, placed a hand on Fenris' fur and asked quietly, "What troubles you, my friend?"

Fenris sighed deeply and began to slowly tell his story. "My father put me on the island," he began. "He told me he put me there for my own safety, but I now know that wasn't the truth."

"Did your father put you on the island?" asked Skrymir.

"Yes, but the memories of him are fading, I remember less and less about him, and where I came from, with each passing hour," said Fenris, depressed.

"But what do you remember?" Skrymir asked, concerned and interested.

Fenris took a deep breath, as if trying to gather his thoughts and emotions, "I remember a place that lies far beyond the simple beauty or splendor here in Jotunheim, a realm of light and greatness, majestic halls that stretch towards the sky like spires of purest gold and silver."

"I remember tall towers that glistened under the eternal sun. Bridges and walkways made of clouds, and rivers flowing with the purest water you can ever imagine."

"But even in this radiance of divinity," Fenris continued, his eyes now darker, "there is a heaviness, a sense of inevitable fates and great responsibilities. It is a place that is both inspiring and frightening, for with great power also comes great trials."

He turned his gaze to Skrymir and continued: "He said it was prophesied that I would do something terrible, something so cruel that it would shake the world. He believed that by isolating me on the island, he could prevent fate from unfolding."

Skrymir listened attentively and placed a comforting hand on Fenris' shoulder. "What do you think, Fenris? Do you really believe you are doomed to fulfill that prophecy?"

Fenris sighed again and shook his head. "No, I don't believe it. I believe we have the power to shape our own destiny, regardless of what has been prophesied about us."

Skrymir smiled encouragingly and said, "You're right, Fenris. You are not bound by the prophecies of the past. You are free to choose your own path and prove that you are more than what was predicted for you."

With these words, Fenris felt a burden lift from his shoulders. He knew he had the power to shape his own future. Together with Skrymir, he would venture out into the world and prove that he was more than just a wolf—he was one destined to create his own fate.

Skrymir looked out over the rolling horizon, where the sun slowly sank behind distant mountains. An evening breeze swept through the forest, and the branches of the trees swayed gently in the wind. By his side sat Fenris, whose eyes followed Skrymir's gaze towards the horizon.

"Fenris, I know someone who might be able to help you," said Skrymir, turning his gaze to the wolf by his side. "Let's go and visit Suttung. He's the wisest I know, he must know where you come from."

Fenris looked puzzled at Skrymir. "Suttung?" "Who is that?" he asked.

Skrymir smiled broadly. "Suttung is an old friend of mine," he explained. "He's a giant, and he always has lots of fun stories to tell."

Fenris' eyes lit up at the thought of meeting a friend. "That sounds exciting!" he exclaimed eagerly. "Let's go right away!"

With a smile, Skrymir rose and stretched lightly. "Let's go, my friend," he said, extending his hand to Fenris. "I'm sure you'll come to like Suttung."

Together, they set off on the path leading to Suttung's mountain. The moon rose in the sky, casting its gentle light over the forest, while the sound of their footsteps soon mingled with the night sounds of the woods.

Suttung's home lay deep in the heart of the forest, surrounded by majestic mountains and enveloped in an aura of mystique. It was a large hut, built into the mountainside with robust timber logs and covered with a thatched roof that almost seemed to blend with the mountain. The light from flaming torches danced on the hut's walls, casting a warm glow over everything.

At the entrance to the hut stood two large, carved wooden posts that seemed to guard the home. A welcome sign, made of colorful feathers and bones, hung from a branch and swayed gently in the wind, which whispered secretive stories through the branches of the trees.

Inside, the hut was filled with coziness. A large fire burned in the middle of the room, its flames casting a warm glow over the walls. The scent of food and drink floated in the air, tickling the nostrils.

Furniture made of rough wood and padded with soft furred skins was scattered around the room, and colorful rugs hung from the walls, adding an ambiance of warmth and coziness. Pictures and artifacts hung everywhere, telling stories of Suttung's life and adventures, and reminding of the many events that had been celebrated here.

All in all, Suttung's home was an oasis of warmth and welcome, a place where friends and acquaintances could gather and share joy and laughter, and where every guest was guaranteed an unforgettable experience.

Suttung was an impressive giant with a stature that filled the room, and a face that bore signs of age and wisdom. His long beard was gray and braided with pearls and stones, symbolizing his connection to the earth and the nature around him. His eyes, deep as the sea and shimmering with wisdom, calmly scanned the assembled guests and radiated an aura of authority and respect.

By his side stood his daughter, Gunlod, a beauty whose face and smile were as enchanting as a starry night. Her long, dark hair flowed down her shoulders in waves, and her eyes, as blue as a clear summer sky, shone with life and youthful exuberance. She wore a dress of precious silk, embroidered with patterns of gold and gemstones that sparkled in the light of the flames.

Suttung and Gunlod made an impressive pair, contrasting each other like day and night, yet united in their love and respect for each other. Together, they represented strength and beauty, wisdom and youth, and their presence filled the room with an aura of magic and mystique that awed and admired their guests.

In the golden glow of the flames, Fenris and Skrymir entered Suttung's home, where an atmosphere of warmth and joy embraced them. Suttung and Gunlod stood by the fire, their smiles wide and welcoming.

"Welcome, my friends!" greeted Suttung with a friendly voice. "We look forward to your company."

Gunlod, with her blue eyes sparkling with curiosity and interest, met Fenris' gaze, and her heart skipped a beat. Never before had she seen such a charming and devoted creature as Fenris, his fur shining in the firelight, and his eyes radiating kindness and love.

"Welcome," she said with a soft voice, almost drowned in a suppressed sigh of admiration.
Inside, the cabin was filled with coziness. A large fire burned in the center of the room, and its flames cast a warm glow over the walls. The scent of food and drink hovered in the air, tickling the nostrils.

The furniture, made of rough wood and upholstered with soft, furry hides, was scattered around the room, while colorful rugs hung from the walls, adding an ambiance of warmth and coziness.
Everywhere, there were pictures and artifacts that told stories of Suttung's life and adventures, reminding of the many events that had been celebrated here.

All in all, Suttung's home was an oasis of warmth and welcome, a place where friends and acquaintances could gather and share joy and laughter, and where each guest was guaranteed an unforgettable experience.

Suttung was an impressive giant with a stature that filled the room, and a face marked by age and wisdom. His long beard was gray and braided with pearls and stones, symbolizing his connection to the earth and the nature around him. His eyes, deep as the ocean and shimmering with wisdom, calmly scanned the assembled guests, radiating an aura of authority and respect.

Beside him stood his daughter, Gunlod,
Fenris noticed her fascination, wagged his tail lightly, and nodded in response. "Thank you," he said with a happy dog-sounding voice that contained joy and warmth.

Skrymir, noticing the immediate connection between the two, smiled mischievously and gave Fenris a discreet nudge with his elbow. "Looks like you've already won her heart," he whispered teasingly.

Fenris couldn't help but wag even more at the thought and turned to Gunlod with a warm smile. "Would you like to go for a walk later," he suggested, and a play of excitement danced in Gunlod's eyes as she accepted with an eager nod.

As the company took their seats at the table in Suttung's cabin, the scent of freshly baked bread and freshly made honey wine filled the air. Suttung and Skrymir sat at the head of the table, while Gunlod and Fenris took their places beside them.

In an atmosphere of coziness and well-being, Skrymir took the floor and began his story. "Yesterday, as I wandered through the forests of Jotunheim, I came upon an island that was sinking. "On the island sat a young wolf cub, lonely and abandoned."

Fenris listened attentively as Skrymir continued. "I knew I had to cross the river to reach it before the island sank, but the current in the water was too strong, and I was not strong enough to swim. But fortunately, a mysterious serpent appeared and offered its help."

" serpent ?" Gunlod exclaimed curiously.

"Yes," confirmed Skrymir and continued: "This serpent was no ordinary serpent . It had the ability to transform and grow in size if it received some magical drink. Together we entered a cave where we stole this drink from a giant spider. With this drink, the serpent gained the power to grow and reach Fenris on the island."

Gunlod's eyes lit up with excitement at the thought of the brave rescue. "So it was the serpent that helped you save him!" she exclaimed gratefully.

Skrymir nodded smilingly. "Yes, it was the serpent that made it possible. He helped us get Fenris to safety."

Suttung and Gunlod also listened attentively to Skrymir's story, impressed by his courage and determination. The mood at the table was filled with gratitude and admiration for the incredible feats that Skrymir and his unusual companion, the serpent , had performed.

Shortly after, Suttung walked through a door and came back with a bottle containing some liquid.

"It seems that such feats should be celebrated," exclaimed Suttung, holding the bottle aloft. He poured four small glasses with the liquid while smiling.

Skrymir and Fenris looked puzzled at the glasses.

"It's not dangerous," Suttung exclaimed with a laugh and drank one of the glasses.

He coughed a bit and exclaimed,

"Do not go gentle into that good night,
Even when age knocks and the day is fading;
Burn up, fight against the dwindling light."

"Wow," said Skrymir, how did you do that?

This is the mead of poetry, Suttung explained, brewed by the dwarves Fjalar and Galar from the honeydew on the shield of the god Kvaser and extracted from the well of wisdom, which the dwarves had killed Kvaser to create.

"Poetry mead," that's incredible, said Skrymir, and picked up a glass to drink.

"Hope is like a little bird,
That lands in the midst of life's tumult,
And sings a quiet song,
That warms the soul and makes it glad.
It is the best guest in stormy weather,
And its song is sweet and soothing,
Even when the world seems most threatening."

Skrymir laughed, try it Fenris. Fenris stood up and went to the glass and drank.

"Some say that the world will end in flames,
Others say that it will be in ice.
If I had to choose, I'd prefer the flames,
But if I had to consider twice,
I know that hate can be just as destructive as fire,
And ice can be just as powerful as fire.
No matter how the world ends, both hate and freezing
Will have their role in its downfall."

"This is the end of everything.
It's obviously the end.
It's the clear end.
We all gather together like a flock of fateful birds towards doomsday."

Suttung laughed, "you are a dark little one," he said and laughed. Fenris looked back embarrassed.

"Suttung?" said Skrymir clearing his throat.

Can you help find out where Fenris comes from?

The four of them sat around the table in Suttung's cabin, where an atmosphere of coziness and well-being prevailed. Its low ceiling and warm burning fire created an atmosphere of safety and togetherness, which Suttung and his daughter, Gunlod, enjoyed along with their guests, Skrymir and Fenris. They shared stories and laughed while sharing food and drink, and everything seemed peaceful and idyllic.

But suddenly, this harmony was broken when the door was kicked open with a violent force that startled everyone. In stepped a tall, impressive figure wearing shining armor and wielding a powerful hammer. It was Brage, the god of poetry and writing, but his face was twisted with anger and hatred.

The silence in the cabin was oppressive, as if the air itself held its breath in anticipation of what would happen next. Brage's gaze was icy and firmly fixed on Fenris, who rose from his seat at the table, ready to defend himself against the sudden threat.

"WOLF!" roared Brage with a voice trembling with rage. "I am the god Brage!" "Offender of fate's fabric,
Your fateful moment is approaching, In your whims is the seed of evil, Your soul bears the burden of chaos and fear."

Fenris looked at Brage with fear in his eyes. Brage shouted again, "Resistance is futile, your fate sealed, In the future, only ruin and death await you, Offender of the gods' patience, Your time has come to pay your debt."

Suttung and Gunlod looked on in shock, their eyes a mix of fear and confusion over the unexpected intrusion of the powerful god. The mood had been replaced by a tense anticipation of what would happen in the next moments.

In the sudden break of harmony and peace, Suttung rose with a will of steel, his eyes filled with a mix of courage and determination as he met Brage's gaze of rage and anger. With a roar of challenge, he lunged at the god, ready for battle.

Brage, the master of war and strife, received Suttung's attack with calm strength. He swung his hammer with ruthless precision, parrying the blows from Suttung with playful ease and retaliating with powerful counterattacks.

In the cutting light from flaming torches, the two warriors danced through the room, their bodies agile and nimble, their weapons smashing together with a resounding crash. Each strike was like a deadly verse in a grim symphony of combat.

Suttung fought with a determination born of millennia of training and experience, but Brage was a god, unmatched in his strength and might. With relentless precision and power, Brage pushed Suttung back, his hammer falling with a terrifying force and hitting Suttung with a powerful thud.

Brage stood before Suttung, triumphantly vanquished by the relentless power of his attack. With a final, radiant burst of triumph, Brage sent Suttung tumbling to the ground, where he lay, defeated and overcome by Brage's unsurpassed strength.

In the moment when the battle between Brage and Suttung raged, Skrymir reached for the bottle with the magical drink. He knew that their only hope was to give Fenris the last magic potion from the Spider's cave.

With a quick movement, Skrymir threw the bottle to Fenris, who caught it in his mouth and drank its contents. Brage looked puzzled at the wolf. Immediately, they could all see the transformation that occurred with the wolf. His eyes glowed with wild energy, and his body pulsed with strength.

With a roar of rage and will, Fenris leaped at Brage with an irresistible force. His muscles were tense, and his teeth sparkled in the cutting light from the flames.

Brage, even a mighty god, could not suppress a stab of fear at the sight of the transformed wolf. He grabbed his hammer and stood ready to fight the raging Fenris.

The battle between the two was epic and violent. Brage, the master of poetry, fought with all his cunning, but Fenris, filled with the magical drink, was invincible. His attacks were wild and unpredictable, and his power was boundless.

Even though Brage fought bravely, he could not withstand Fenris' irresistible rage. With a final roar of triumph, Fenris lunged at the god and crushed him with a powerful wave of strength.

Suttung and Skrymir looked on in shock as the battle unfolded before their eyes. They knew they were witnessing an epic confrontation between two powerful beings.

In the blazing inferno of battle's wildness, Fenris lunged at Brage with a terrifying strength, his jaws wide open like a predator, ready to crush the god with a single bite. Brage, seized by fear and anger, tried to defend himself with his hammer, but he was overwhelmed by Fenris' invincible power.

With a roar of victory, Fenris crushed Brage with tremendous force, and the god fell to the ground with a crash. Fenris' triumphant roar filled the hut, and Suttung and Skrymir watched in shock as the battle reached its dramatic conclusion.

As Brage lay defeated on the floor, he slowly rose, his face twisted with pain and defeat. With a voice filled with hatred and desperation, he revealed his true intent.

"Fenris," said Brage, his voice trembling with rage and scorn, "I came to kill you and steal the poetic elixir. But now I see that you have underestimated me."

Fenris looked at Brage with a mix of contempt and pity. He knew that the god was an enemy, but he couldn't help feeling a pang of pity for him.

"You have failed, Brage," Fenris said with a voice exuding authority and strength. "You underestimated our strength and will to fight for what we believe in. Now it is time for you to leave this hut and never return."

Defeated and humiliated, Brage left the hut with one last glance at Fenris and his allies. He knew he had underestimated them, and that they were stronger than he had ever imagined.

"Skrymir and Fenris," said Suttung with awe in his voice, "I would like to thank you both for your courage and determination in the fight against Brage. Without you, we would not have survived this day."

Gunhild nodded in agreement and added with a smile: "Truly, you have proven yourselves as real heroes. Your will and strength have saved us all from a fate worse than death."

Fenris and Skrymir received Suttung's and Gunhild's gratitude with humility and appreciation. Although they were not accustomed to praise or acclaim, it was a feeling of pride and joy that filled their hearts.

"We better head home," said Skrymir, looking at Fenris. "Yes," sighed Fenris. "Gunhild, would you like me to sleep at your place?" "I'm a bit too tired after the battle," said Fenris, "I'll probably sleep outside; I don't know how big I'll get."

After the intense battle and victory over Brage, Fenris and Skrymir returned to the hut. They entered the safe space, filled with warmth and tranquility. The heavy fog of fatigue settled over them, and they both headed to their beds with a relief only felt after a hard-won victory.

With a final look at each other, radiating both strength and camaraderie, they lay down and closed their eyes, ready to rest after the day's challenges. The hut's walls were filled with the deep breath of silence, and in the darkness, they both fell into a peaceful sleep, dreaming of tomorrow's adventures.

Chapter 3: The Eagle's Battle

The next day, Fenris and Skrymir woke up in the cabin and decided to return to Suttung's cabin to thank him and Gunhild for their hospitality and to discuss the events of the previous day.

On their way through the forest, the mood was light and relaxed. Sunbeams danced between the treetops, and the birds' singing filled the air with a lively symphony. Fenris and Skrymir shared laughs and fond memories from the day before, their steps light and carefree.

Upon reaching the cabin, they were greeted by Gunhild, who was waiting at the door. Their faces showed confusion and disappointment.

"Fenris, Skrymir!" Gunhild greeted them with a warm embrace. "We have been deceived."

In the dim light of Suttung's cabin, Gunhild stood astonished as she shared her experience with Fenris and Skrymir.

Odin, the cunning and powerful king of the gods, had visited and tricked them in a way they could never have imagined.

"It's incredible," exclaimed Fenris, a mix of fascination and wonder in his voice. "Odin himself came here and deceived you?"

Skrymir nodded in agreement, his thoughts swirling as he tried to grasp the extensive consequences of Odin's actions.

Gunhild sighed deeply, her face twisted with disappointment and anger. "I thought the serpent that tempted me to share the potion with him was your friend, the one who helped save you, Fenris," she explained. "But it was Odin who deceived me with his powerful transformation."

"He drank all the potion," she continued, "and recited this poem before he transformed and fled:

In the dark depths of Yggdrasil's womb,
Where worlds meet and fates are tied,
There I travel, with the raven's cry,
On a quest for wisdom and the realms divine.

I wander through shadow and light,
Through realms of ice and fire,
I meet giants and elves, in the name of truth,
And drank from the spring where wisdom flows.

From the Heavens in the north to Helheim's depths,
From Midgard's fields to the ocean's foam,
He beheld the cosmos with eyes of amber,
And sang his wise songs to the world's acclaim.

My words are like runes, engraved in time,
My voice like the wind, that whispers by,

Here is a gift of wisdom, a gift to Suttung,
In exchange for the drink that awakens the mind.

Listen to my song, you who wish to understand,
For in each verse lies a secret so grand,
About the world's beginning and the night of the end,
About the power of love and the call of fate.

Gunhild's face was marked by deep seriousness as she continued her story. "When we discovered the deceit, my father, Suttung, became so enraged that he took his true form as a mighty eagle and pursued Odin.

I hurried up the mountain, following them as far as I could. You should have seen their chase; it was fierce. The sky darkened, like a storm breaking loose over Jotunheim.

Fenris and Skrymir listened intently, their eyes reflecting the excitement and awe that Gunhild's words evoked. "Suttung soared through the clouds with a speed that could split the air," she continued. "He was a fearsome sight to behold, his wings stretched out like shadows covering the sun."
"Odin, for his part, was not easy to capture. He used his cunning and magical abilities to evade Suttung, changing form and disappearing into the mists, only to reappear far away. It was like a game between two mighty forces, where each maneuver and each dive was filled with an intensity that could be felt all the way down to the earth."

Gunhild's eyes sparkled with a mix of pride and concern as she described her father's heroic efforts. "Although Suttung is strong and fearless, Odin was just as cunning as he is powerful. The chase continued across the sky, a dance between eagle and god, until they finally vanished on the horizon."

She sighed deeply, and a silence settled over the group as they digested the story of the divine pursuit. "What am I to do without my father, he should have been home long ago," added Gunhild with a sad tone.

Fenris and Skrymir exchanged worried glances, aware that they had

been drawn into a battle between titans, where the future was uncertain and filled with both danger and opportunities.
Why on earth would he steal the potion?" Fenris asked, puzzled.

With a trembling voice, Gunhild added, "It must have been Brage who sent him. We were deceived by the cunning king of the gods, and now the potion, meant to be a gift for Jotunheim, has vanished forever."

For Suttung and Gunhild, the loss of the poetic potion had far-reaching consequences, extending beyond the confines of their humble dwelling. The potion, intended as a divine gift, was taken from them due to Odin's deceit.

As guardians of the magical brew, Suttung and Gunhild had hoped to use its power to usher in a new era of wisdom and happiness in Jotunheim. The potion had been a source of inspiration and joy for both, and they had looked forward to sharing its magic with their people.

Now, with the potion gone and no hope of retrieving it, Suttung and Gunhild felt powerless and disillusioned. Without the potion, their dreams of a better future for their land and people would never materialize.

Gunhild sighed heavily, her face twisted with disappointment and sorrow. She knew she must now face her fate without her father and the magical drink, a thought that filled her with a deep sense of loss and emptiness.

Fenris and Skrymir exchanged worried glances as they grasped the severe consequences of Odin's deceit. They knew they had to act quickly to reclaim Suttung and the potion from Odin.

Skrymir looked at Fenris: "We cannot let this happen," he said, his voice carrying both strength and underlying anger. "We must go to Asgard and get Suttung and the potion back."

Fenris nodded, his sturdy frame tense in agreement. He took a deep breath and looked at Skrymir. "We need to find Odin and demand he return the potion and Suttung. It's our only chance to correct this injustice."

"It will be dangerous," Gunhild objected, her brows furrowed in concern. "Odin is not one to easily relinquish what he has taken. You must be wise and strong."

Skrymir placed a hand on Gunhild's shoulder, a gesture of both gratitude and camaraderie. "Odin must be reasoned with," he said calmly, seeming to reassure them both. "And we have the power of justice on our side. Together, we can do this."

"Will you stay a bit longer?" Gunhild asked.

Skrymir and Fenris stayed a while to comfort Gunhild but soon had to leave to retrieve the potion and Suttung from Odin.

With quiet determination, Fenris and Skrymir left Suttung's mountain hut into the now dark night, their minds set on confronting Odin, whatever it might require. Skrymir quietly wondered to himself how one could stand against a god as mighty and cunning as Odin.

In the silent darkness, where stars cast their glow through the tall treetops, Skrymir and Fenris set out into the night, through Jotunheim's dense forests. The leaves rustled like whispering spirits, and shadows danced under the pale moonlight.

Fenris's yellow eyes shone like glowing fire in the dark, and his steps were strong and sure, as if he knew the way through the forest's dense labyrinth of trees and bushes. Skrymir, his companion, followed closely, his heart filled with a mix of excitement and awe at being in this enchanted world.

They walked through the forest, listening to the sounds of the night's life singing in the forest's depths. An owl hooted its melancholy song, and a bat flew silently by. Each step took them deeper into the heart of the forest, where secrets and mysteries awaited revelation.

Suddenly, Fenris stopped and lifted his head, his ears pricked as if listening to a distant melody. "What is that?" Skrymir asked, his voice whispering in the quiet night.

Fenris didn't respond, but his eyes glowed with a kind of inner knowledge. He began moving forward again, and Skrymir followed, wondering what awaited them ahead in the depths of the forest.

Deep in Jotunheim's forests, where the branches of the trees twisted like gnarled fingers against the sky, Skrymir and Fenris quietly moved through the darkness. The pale moonlight cast ghostly shadows over the path, and the sound of their footsteps was lost in the forest's dense fog.

Suddenly, as they rounded a bend, they came upon a small clearing where a faint fire burned, casting its glowing light into the darkness. By the fire sat an old woman, wrapped in a dried pelt, staring into the flames with cloudy eyes. It must have been her that Fenris had detected, Skrymir thought to himself.

Skrymir and Fenris paused and observed her with curiosity. "Good evening," Skrymir said politely as he stepped closer. "What brings you to these woods?"

The old woman slowly raised her head and met their gaze with a hint of surprise in her tired eyes. "Evening," she replied with a trembling voice. "I am just a wanderer seeking shelter and warmth on this cold night."

Fenris, intrigued by the old woman's presence, stepped closer and studied her intently. "What are you doing here alone?" he asked, his voice filled with curiosity.

The old woman smiled faintly and shook her head. "I have wandered these woods for years, my young friend," she answered in a wondrous tone. "I seek answers to questions that only nature can provide."

Skrymir and Fenris listened patiently to the old woman's words, the sense of mystique enveloping her like a fog. What was her story, and what was her purpose in this forest's solitude? These were questions that only time could reveal.

The old woman sat by the fire, the flames dancing in her cloudy eyes, as memories from a distant past surged forth.

She told of a time when the world was young, and the forests were filled with magic and mysteries. She was once a proud giantess princess, daughter of a mighty giant king, and she roamed the forests freely, enchanted by nature's beauty and power.

But fate turned when a war broke out between the gods and the giants, and her homeland was laid to ruin. Her father fell in battle, and her people were scattered to the wind like leaves in autumn's storms. She was left alone and lost in a world that had become alien to her.

"Long ago, when the world was young and its fate still being shaped, a conflict of great significance arose," the old lady began, her voice filled with weight and experience. "It was a war between the gods, who ruled from Asgard, and the giants, whose power lay in Jotunheim."

She continued to paint a vivid picture of the epic battles that took place on the battlefields, where gods and giants stood face to face in a struggle for the fate of the world. "Thor swung his hammer, Mjolnir, with powerful blows, while Odin fought with wisdom and cunning. On the other side stood giant rulers like the feared Surt, king of the fire giants, and the mighty Farbauti, king of the ice giants, whose powers challenged even the strongest of gods."

"The battles were intense and fierce," she continued, "with fire, lightning, and thunder breaking out in the sky as manifestations of the war's fury. Gods and giants fought with everything they had, in an attempt to gain control over the world order and the fate of all living beings."

"One of the most memorable battles during the war between gods and giants was the epic duel between Thor, the mighty warlord of the gods, and Surt, one of the most feared giant rulers," the old lady began, her voice filled with excitement and awe.

She described the scene before them with vivid details: Thor, standing tall and strong with his golden hammer, Mjolnir, in hand, while Surt, a colossus of a giant, raised his enormous sword of fire and let out a furious roar.

"It was as if the sky itself shook with fear as Thor and Thrym collided," she continued, "lightning flew from Mjolnir, while Thrym's sword cut through the air with powerful blows. Each strike, each thrust, was met with strength and determination, as two titans fought for dominance."

She described Thor's courage, his unmatched strength and fighting skills, and Thrym's brutality and relentless anger. "It was a battle that would be remembered for all eternity," she said, "for it was here, among the battlefields, that the fate of the gods was shaped by the will to fight and win."

Finally, with a deep sigh of relief, she explained how it was Thor who ultimately triumphed over Thrym, and how his victory marked a turning point in the war between gods and giants. "But even though Thor won that day," she said with a tone of seriousness, "the memory of the battle and its significance will remain engraved in our hearts and minds forever."

Finally, with a tone of melancholy, the old lady explained how it was the gods who ultimately triumphed and established their dominion over the world order. "But even though the war between gods and giants ended, the conflict between order and chaos continues to shape our world and our fate," she said, letting the significance of the story sink in. "It is a struggle that will always be remembered and carried forward in our hearts and minds, even as time flows like the river and memories fade like leaves on trees."

To avoid the wrath of the gods and persecution, she transformed her form and hid deep in the forest, where she lived as a simple wanderer. She concealed her memories and true identity behind a facade of old age and wisdom, and she still sought answers to the questions that burned in her soul.

Through the centuries, she wandered alone through the forests, observing and listening to nature's wisdom. She became a wandering history book, bearing secrets and tales from a time that had been lost to oblivion.
Although she was alone, she never felt lonely, for she was surrounded by trees, plants, and animals that shared their secrets with her. She was a part of the forest, and the forest was a part of her. However, beneath the old woman's dried fur and foggy eyes lay a hidden wisdom and cunning that only a few could recognize.

After listening to stories and exchanging experiences for a while, Skrymir stepped forward. "We seek Odin of Asgard," he declared. "Can you help us find the way to his realm?"

The woman nodded slowly with a smile on her lips. "Yes, I know a man at the end of Jotunheim who can lead you to Asgard," she said. "But the path is not easy, and the price is high."

Skrymir and Fenris listened intently, their interest piqued by the woman's words. "What is the price?" Skrymir asked.

The woman pointed toward the depths of the forest. "There is an apple orchard somewhere in Jotunheim, guarded by a wight," she explained. "I know the gate to Asgard, but only if you bring me an apple from the Wight's orchard. It is a task that requires bravery and cunning, but the reward is great."

Fenris furrowed his brows in wonder and asked, "Who are these wights you speak of? And why are their apples so important?"

The old woman took a deep breath and straightened up in her chair, her eyes gleaming with wisdom that seemed to extend far beyond the forest's boundaries. "The wights," she began, "are ancient beings, deeply rooted in the soil and nature of Jotunheim. They are not only guardians of the apple orchard but also keepers of magical secrets and ancient powers woven into the very land."

"Each apple in their orchard contains a part of this magic, an essence of Jotunheim's ancient strength. To possess such an apple is to hold a part of this world's power in your hands," she continued.

Skrymir and Fenris exchanged a look, this time filled with determination. "We accept the challenge," declared Skrymir. "We will find the apples and bring them to you, so we can travel to Asgard."

The old lady, her face weathered by time, stared into the flames with a crooked smile on her lips. "Thank you for your courage and willingness to find the apples," she said with a voice carrying wisdom and secrets from bygone times. "But before you continue on your journey, would you like to solve a riddle?"

With these words, she pulled out a bottle from her cloak, its glass shining in the moonlight. "This is a potion," she continued, "that can aid you on your way. But only if you manage to solve the riddle that guards its contents."

Skrymir and Fenris listened attentively, their eyes filled with anticipation and curiosity. "What is the riddle?" asked Fenris.

The old lady smiled mysteriously and began:

"I am light as a feather, yet even the strongest cannot hold me.
I am invisible as the wind, yet you can feel my touch.
I flee from those who chase me, but to those who seek me, I am easy to find.
What am I?"

Skrymir and Fenris looked at each other, deeply immersed in thought as they tried to solve the riddle that would determine their fate and open the way to the magical potion. "What could the answer be?"

After a moment of silence, they rose from the fire, ready to give up. But just before they left, Skrymir cast one last glance at the flames and noticed something strange. He saw his own shadow dancing on the ground, created by the warm glow of the fire.

Suddenly, his face lit up with understanding, and he exclaimed, "The shadow! The answer to the riddle is the shadow!"

The old lady smiled as if she had been waiting for this moment. Without a word, she tossed the potion to them, and the bottle glided through the air until Skrymir caught it.

"Take this with you on your journey," said the old lady with a voice filled with magic and secrets. "May it lead you to the wisdom you seek and protect you on your way."

With the bottle safely in their possession, Skrymir and Fenris set their course towards the unknown, ready to face the challenges and adventures that lay ahead.

Chapter 4: The Apple Tree

Skrymir and Fenris continued their journey through the forest, eventually reaching a clearing that opened up to vast fields. They paused to admire the fields where the sun's rays danced upon the soft grass and the wind caressed the landscape with playful ease. Ahead of them lay a small village of caves embedded in the hills and cliffs, as if sculpted by nature's own hands.

The caves stretched into the mountainsides, serving as protective shelters that offered safety and comfort to the villagers. Giants and Vættir moved about, with children playing and laughing, and adults attending to their daily chores.

Skrymir and Fenris walked along the narrow paths between the caves, their feet easily finding their way on the rocky ground, their minds filled with curiosity and anticipation. They greeted the villagers with smiles and kind words, feeling immediately welcomed in this natural and rustic corner of the world.

As the day progressed, they enjoyed the village's hospitality and beauty, watching the sun slowly sink below the horizon, casting a golden glow over everything. They knew they had found a special place, an oasis of peace amidst a world filled with strife and chaos.

As the sun dipped below the horizon, painting the sky in warm shades of orange and purple, Skrymir and Fenris realized it was time to find a place to rest. Their weary feet trudged along the paths, searching for a spot to camp for the night.

The surrounding landscape was calm and quiet, with only the sound of the wind rustling through the trees breaking the silence. Eventually, they came upon a small inn by the roadside, its cozy atmosphere radiating through the windows and door.

The inn's facade was rustic and charming, constructed of wood and stone and illuminated by the gentle light of lanterns outside. A smoking chimney emitted the scent of warm food, making their stomachs rumble with hunger.

With smiles on their faces, they entered the inn, where they were immediately greeted by the warmth of the fireplace and the hum of voices and laughter. The innkeeper, a friendly and welcoming figure, greeted them with open arms and showed them to a table by the fire.

They settled into their chairs, enjoying the warmth of the flames as they ordered a meal and a place to rest their heads for the night. The inn was filled with travelers and locals sharing stories around the tables, the atmosphere brimming with kindness and camaraderie.

In the cozy inn, where the flames from the fireplace cast a warm glow on the walls, Skrymir and Fenris savored a delicious meal, their bellies happy and satisfied. However, despite the warmth and lively conversations, Skrymir couldn't help but think about how they could find the Vættir the old lady had told them about.

"Skrymir," Fenris suddenly said, turning to his companion, "where do we find the Vættir the old lady asked us about? Perhaps the innkeeper knows where they are."

Skrymir nodded thoughtfully. "That sounds like a good idea, Fenris. Let's ask the innkeeper if she knows where we can find the Vættir ."

With that, Skrymir rose from the table and approached the innkeeper, who was busy arranging beer mugs at the counter. "Excuse me, ma'am," Skrymir began politely, "but we're looking for some Vættir . Do you know where we can find them? We need their help to find some special apples for an elderly lady."

The innkeeper, a friendly woman with a smiling face, thought for a moment. "I know where the Vættir dwell," she replied, "and I can tell you if you can drink a mug of beer."

"A mug of beer, easily!" exclaimed Skrymir with a smile.

Skrymir and Fenris thanked her for her help and returned to their table, excited about the upcoming meeting with the Vættir . They knew it would be an important part of their journey to find the apples for the old lady, and they were determined to do their best to succeed.

In the warm and lively inn, the innkeeper came down to the table, carrying a mug of beer so full it almost overflowed. "Here is your beer, gentlemen," she said with a smile, placing the mug in front of Skrymir and Fenris.

Skrymir immediately grabbed the mug and lifted it to his lips, expecting it to be an easy task. But no matter how much he drank, the amount in the mug seemed not to decrease. He drank and drank until he was quite dizzy. Confused and surprised, he set it back on the table and looked questioningly at the innkeeper.

The innkeeper couldn't hold back her laughter as she saw Skrymir's puzzled expression. "What's wrong?" he asked, puzzled by the strange behavior of the beer.

The innkeeper exploded with laughter "It's an old giant trick, gentlemen," the innkeeper explained between fits of laughter. "The mug is enchanted and connected to the stream out front. No matter how much you drink, the contents will never disappear. It's a joke we love to play on unsuspecting travelers."

Skrymir and Fenris couldn't help but laugh at the funny situation, sharing a look of understanding. "That was a good one," Skrymir admitted, wiping tears of laughter from his eyes. "I must admit my defeat. It seems we'll have to try to find the Vættir in another way."

With laughter still ringing in the inn, the innkeeper returned to the bar. "What should we do, Skrymir?" Fenris asked.

"I don't know, should we go up and sleep, and then figure it out tomorrow?" Skrymir replied.

As they rose to leave, an impressive giant stepped forward before Skrymir and Fenris, its figure filled with an aura of mystique and power. "Listen, travelers," the giant said in a deep voice that resonated through the inn. "I know where you can find the Vættir if you are willing to take on a challenge."

Skrymir and Fenris exchanged a look of curiosity and interest. "What kind of challenge are you talking about?" Skrymir asked.

The giant smiled slyly and replied, "I challenge you to a duel in Hnefatafl, the king's board game. If you win, I will show you the way to the realm of the Vættir, where you can find what you seek."

"What is Hnefatafl?" Fenris asked. Skrymir explained that Hnefatafl is an exciting ancient board game where two teams battle each other. One team consists of the king and his defenders, while the other team are the attackers trying to capture the king.

"We place our pieces on a board with an odd number of squares. The king starts in the middle, surrounded by his defenders, while the attackers are placed along the edge of the board. The goal for the attackers is to capture the king by surrounding him on two opposite sides. Our task as defenders is to protect the king and prevent the attackers from reaching him. The pieces move like chess pieces, but the king can only move one square at a time. We must think strategically and tactically to win this exciting game!"

"I don't understand much of that," said Fenris, "I've never played board games before. I don't even think I can move the small pieces with my paws." Skrymir looked surprised at Fenris, "Look up at the wall, the rules are there," said Skrymir.
Fenris looked up at the wall and whispered to himself, "Rules of Hnefatafl."

1. Objective: The game has two teams - defenders and attackers. The defenders' goal is to protect the king, while the attackers aim to capture him.

2. Board: The board is a square grid, typically 11x11, 13x13, or 19x19 squares. The king is placed in the center, surrounded by his defenders. The attackers start at the edges of the board.

3. Pieces: The defenders consist of the king and several defensive pieces. The attackers have more pieces than the defenders.

4. Movement: Pieces move horizontally or vertically across the squares like chess pieces. The king can only move one square at a time.

5. Capture: A piece is captured when it is trapped between two enemy pieces either horizontally or vertically.

6. Victory: The defenders win if the king reaches one of the four corners of the board. The attackers win if they can surround the king on two opposite sides.

7. Starting Positions: The defenders place the king in the center with defenders around him. The attackers place their pieces along the board's edge.

8. Turns: The defenders move first, followed by the attackers. Turns alternate until the game ends.

9. Special Rules: There are various versions of Hnefatafl with additional rules and varying board sizes.

Skrymir and Fenris exchanged a determined look and accepted the challenge. The board was set up, and the game began. Skrymir, with his sharp intelligence and tactical acumen, led the team.
The giant proved to be a formidable opponent, and the game quickly filled with excitement and intensity. Pieces were moved with deep concentration and strategic consideration, as victory hung in the balance.

Skrymir and the giant fought hard to gain the upper hand, but it was Skrymir who, with ingenious tactics and courage, managed to trap the giant's king in a cunning snare. With a triumphant smile, Skrymir declared victory and proved himself the master of Hnefatafl.

Although the giant acknowledged his defeat, he honestly respected the agreement. "You have won," the giant acknowledged. "Well played, young Skrymir. My name is Thorgar. I will keep my promise. The path to the realm of the spirits lies before you."
"Thank you, Thorgar, you are the best I have ever played against," said Skrymir.

In the quiet embrace of twilight, Skrymir and Fenris retreated to their bed in the small inn. After a long day filled with challenges and planning, the bed felt like a welcome oasis of rest.

The moon cast its gentle light through the window, bathing the room in a silvery glow. Skrymir lay down on the simple straw bed and let out a sigh of relief. He could feel the fatigue in his muscles, but also a bubbling excitement for the coming day.

Fenris found his resting place at Skrymir's feet, curling up like a protective guard. His eyes mirrored the same anticipation and a loyal devotion to his companion.

As they slowly drifted into the realm of dreams, the inn was filled with a deep silence, only interrupted by the sounds of the night outside. For Skrymir and Fenris, it was a moment of peace and tranquility amidst their journey through Jotunheim, a pause before facing new challenges and adventures in the morning light.

As morning broke with its gentle light, Skrymir and Fenris woke to the sound of a deep and powerful voice filling the inn. It was Thorgar, the mighty giant, standing at the door, ready to start their journey.
With a strong and authoritative voice, Thorgar shouted, "Wake up, travelers! The time has come to begin our journey to the realm of the spirits."

Skrymir and Fenris immediately sprang up from their bed, awakened by Thorgar's powerful words. They felt a wave of excitement invigorate their minds as they prepared for what lay ahead.

With quick and decisive movements, they readied themselves to leave the inn and embark on the next part of their journey. Thorgar led the way with firm steps, and Skrymir and Fenris followed in his footsteps, ready to face the challenges that awaited them on their journey through Jotunheim.

As Thorgar led the way back into the forest, Skrymir and Fenris followed closely behind, their steps muffled by the dense foliage covering the path. The forest opened up to them like an enchanted realm, where sunbeams filtered through the treetops and cast a pattern of light and shadow on the soft forest floor.

Along the way, they could hear the rustling of leaves in the wind and the sound of birdsong filling the forest with life and motion. Thorgar led them deeper and deeper into the forest, through winding paths and dense vegetation, following the trail that led them to the realm of the spirits.

As they continued their journey, they could feel a tension of anticipation growing in the air, as if the forest itself was alive with the expectation of their arrival. Skrymir and Fenris felt uplifted by the magical atmosphere around them, ready to meet the spirits that awaited them and solve the challenges that lay ahead on their journey through Jotunheim.
Skrymir, Fenris, and Thorgar sat down and began to converse with the king, sharing their adventures and hopes for the future. In the heart of the wight's palace, they felt welcomed and respected.

Skrymir expressed their desire to obtain some apples, explaining to the wight king that they had promised to help an old lady acquire them. The wight king listened attentively and nodded understandingly before he began to explain the special significance of the apples.

"These apples, my friends," the wight king started in a deep voice, "are no ordinary fruits. They are a source of wisdom and strength, accessible only to those brave enough to seek them." He described how the apples contained powerful magic that could bring balance and peace to those who recognized their true value.

"The old lady you mentioned," the wight king continued, "is she a cherished guardian of the apples' wisdom? Will she watch over them carefully and use their powers to strengthen and heal?"
"Yes, I am sure of it," replied Skrymir. "The old woman roams around Jotunheim, and she just wants to use some of the apples so she can continue her wanderings."

The king nodded with a smile of understanding. "You are welcome to try and pick the apples, but don't be surprised if you are unable to. Very few have been permitted to harvest them."

The wight king led Skrymir, Fenris, and Thorgar through the wight's city and out into the deep forests stretching along the valley. They walked through dense trees and fragrant flowers until they reached a secluded area where a majestic tree stood alone amid the forest's glow.

The tree, a radiant gem among the green surroundings, was nothing short of breathtaking. Its branches were laden with beautiful, red apples that shone like jewels in the sunlight. The leaves surrounding the tree were a deep green, and their gentle movements in the wind gave the tree an almost magical aura.

The wight king stopped in front of the tree and turned to Skrymir, Fenris, and Thorgar with a smile. "Here is the apple tree," he declared proudly, gesturing towards its beauty. "Its fruits contain wisdom and strength, but can only be picked by those who are brave and true of heart. We need to pick some apples for the town today, so give it a try."

Skrymir, Fenris, and Thorgar stared in awe at the tree and its golden apples, deeply moved by the sight. They now understood why the apples were so precious, and they promised each other to protect them with all their strength and loyalty.

With a nod, the wight king left them to their task. Skrymir, Fenris, and Thorgar stood still for a moment, contemplating the apple tree, filled with gratitude and awe, before they attempted to pick the apples and fulfill their mission.

Chapter 5: The Apples

Skrymir, accompanied by Fenris, ventured to where the magical apple tree stood, swaying in the wind like a living fountain of life and youth. The tree's branches bore apples of the purest colors and glowing beauty, their fragrance filling the air with an enchanting aroma.

With awe and respect, Skrymir approached the tree, admiring its beauty with wonder. He understood the value and significance of the apples for both gods and humans and felt a deep respect for this sacred place.

Gently, Skrymir began to pick the apples one by one from the tree's lavish branches. His hands handled them with care and reverence, as if they were precious jewels needing cautious handling.

Fenris, standing by his side, observed the beauty of the apples with a mix of curiosity and awe.

Together, they filled their baskets with the magical apples, radiating with the essence of life and youth. As Skrymir picked the apples, he felt as though he was experiencing something sacred and transcendent, something that would be engraved in his heart forever.

Suddenly, the atmosphere filled with tension and confusion. In the midst of their apple-picking, Skrymir and Fenris were startled by a scream that pierced the air.

They turned around to see the sprite king lying on the ground, stabbed from behind, his face expressing pain and surprise. Beside him stood Idun and Brage, her eyes blazing with anger and determination, still holding the knife that had performed the deadly act.

Skrymir and Fenris stared in shock, astonished by the unexpected attack. Idun, usually associated with beauty, youth, and fertility, now seemed enveloped in an aura of formidable strength and vengeance.

Brage stepped forward, his voice calm but with an undertone of firm resolve. "For many years, we have sought the magical apples that can restore youth and strength to Asgard. Our world has suffered under the burden of aging, and without these apples, even the mightiest among us will fade and lose their power."

He looked down at the sprite king, who lay motionless. "The sprite king has hidden the location of the apples over time, using them to manipulate and maintain his own power. His greed and fear of losing control have cost us dearly. We could no longer stand by and watch our people suffer."

Idun stepped closer, still holding the knife. "The apples belong not to one, but to all in Asgard. By restoring access to them, we can secure a future full of vitality and strength for our home. It was a difficult decision, but necessary."

Thorgar, a proud and fearless warrior, stepped forward with clenched fists and a face burning with anger and courage. He stared deeply into Brage's eyes, ready to face the evil head-on, in a battle against the enemy that had now brought destruction and suffering.

Brage took a defensive stance, his body tense in anticipation of the inevitable clash. He knew this confrontation would be crucial for his plans to procure the apples for his beloved Idun, so he was determined to defend himself against Thorgar's attack.

With a sudden move, Thorgar stepped closer, his fists clenched ready for battle, but before he could strike, he was hit by Brage's swift hammer, sending him tumbling to the ground.

Thorgar, writhing in pain and regret, felt the ground give way beneath him as he struggled to rise, ready to continue the fight. He couldn't; it was as if the blow was magical, he usually wasn't knocked out by a single strike.

Brage now stood over Thorgar, his gaze both triumphant and evil. There was a clear, deep connection to the ancient feud between gods and giants that had smoldered through the centuries.

Suddenly, Brage lifted his gaze. His eyes gleamed evilly. Opposite him stood Skrymir, determined to prevent Brage and Idun from stealing the life-giving apples. Without these apples, they would be unable to reach Asgard.

Like lightning from a clear sky, Brage sprinted towards Skrymir. With a thunderous crash, the two mighty opponents met, and their battle filled the air with lightning and thunder, breaking the otherwise quiet forest. Brage, armed with his sharp sword and magical powers, attacked with relentless intensity. Skrymir, with his raw strength and bravery, parried with all his might.

Each blow and each parry sent shockwaves through the forest, and the ground shook under their feet. Brage, driven by his greed and ambitions, hurled enchanted curses at Skrymir, who stood firm and refused to yield.

But Skrymir, with his strong will and unshakeable faith, fought back with all his strength and resistance. He withstood Brage's attacks with impressive resilience, and even as blows rained down around him, he refused to bow to the will of evil.

In the roaring battle between Skrymir and Brage, as thunder rolled and lightning flamed, With lightning speed, he ran towards the battleground, his paws hammering against the ground, and his eyes flaming with determination.

But in the midst of his fierce run, Fenris suddenly felt a sharp pain piercing through his side. Idun, driven by the lust for evil, had sneaked close and stabbed a poisonous knife into his side, in an attempt to weaken the brave wolf and disrupt his advance.

Fenris' roar filled the forest as the pain sliced through his body, and his steps weakened, but his will remained unyielding. With one last effort, he continued his run, his stride strong and his eyes burning with determination. He reached the battleground just in time, and his presence gave Skrymir a new wave of strength and resistance.

Idun's cowardly act was met with fury from Skrymir and a rallying of support from the brave warriors' side. Even though Fenris' fight had been complicated by the vile attack, he refused to be stopped by anything, and he stood firm by Skrymir's side, ready to fight against the forces of evil until the last breath.

With a deep sigh, Fenris let himself sink to the ground, his large body resting against the cool, damp substrate. His eyes slowly closed, and his breathing became deeper and more regular as he fell into a deep sleep.

While Fenris slept, the battle between Skrymir and the evil forces, Brage and Idun, intensified. Skrymir, exhausted but unyielding, faced the two opponents with impressive strength and resilience. He fought them with a fire in his heart and a determination in his eyes that could not be shaken by even the most terrible attacks.

Brage and Idun, driven by their lust for evil and their desire to see Jotunheim fall, attacked with all their power and cunning, but Skrymir refused to yield. He stood firm as a mountain in the storm, and although the fight was tough and exhausting, he refused to bow to the will of evil.

Idun and Brage, driven by their will for evil and the desire to dominate, continued their relentless attacks against Skrymir. Although the brave giant stood firm as a mountain wall, he was ultimately unable to withstand the endless pressure from the forces of evil.

Brage, with his cunning attacks and sharp sword, managed to penetrate Skrymir's defense, and Idun, with her treacherous knife and cunning tactics, found weaknesses in his combat strategy. Together, the two forces of evil worked in a perfectly synchronized dance of destruction and chaos.

Skrymir, exhausted and wounded, fought bravely, but even his strongest efforts were not enough to fend off the terrible attack. With a last roar of resistance, he was overwhelmed by the superior power of the gods, and he sank to the ground, overcome and defeated.

Idun and Brage, triumphant over their victory, raised their weapons and laughed in triumph as they looked down at the fallen giant. Their plans had succeeded, and now nothing was left to prevent them from achieving their goal.

Idun, bending down over the fallen Skrymir, whispered with a hint of compassion in her voice. "Giant," she began, her voice a gentle breeze in the dim forest, "you may wonder why we were so determined to get these apples." A moment of contemplation filled her gaze before she continued, "It's because these apples possess a power that is necessary to save our home, Asgard."

She let her fingertips brush the golden apples scattered around them, and her eyes filled with deep sorrow. "I have asked the king many times to get just one apple, but he stubbornly refuses each time. I did not want to steal them, but time is short, and our home faces a threat that only these apples can counter."

Idun's voice carried a heavy burden of responsibility and concern. "I ask you to understand. I do not wish to harm or diminish Jotunheim in any way. I only seek to save our worlds from doom."

With the words about the apples' true purpose still hanging in the air, Idun and Brage disappeared into the night's depths like a pair of shadows merging with the darkness. Their figures gradually blurred by the dense trees and the faint glimmers of stars until they were completely gone, leaving Skrymir alone in the forest's silence. A feeling of loss rested heavily on him as he lay there among the apple tree's shadowy silhouette, while the night's cold penetrated his bones.

With a hand trembling slightly from effort and concern, Skrymir gently pulled out the bottle of magic potion from his belt. The old woman's words about the potion and its healing properties still echoed in his mind, like a faint encouragement in the darkness. With a decisive nod, he removed the cork and let the golden liquid slide down his throat.

A moment of anticipation and excitement filled the air around him as he felt the potion slowly spread through his body. A renewed sense of strength and vitality flowed through him, and the fatigue that had weighed on his shoulders was gradually replaced by a newfound energy. Skrymir felt his heart beat stronger, and his muscles felt firm and strong again.

With a relieved sigh and a grateful smile, Skrymir stood up. Skrymir approached Thorgar and Fenris with calm determination. He first handed the bottle to Thorgar and then to Fenris, one after the other. With a smile on his lips and a glint of anticipation in his eyes, they each took a sip of the golden liquid.

A wave of revitalization washed over their bodies, and the fatigue disappeared like dew in the sun. The energy and zest for life returned to them, and they immediately felt stronger and more awake.
Skrymir then went to the king, who lay completely unconscious. He poured a little magic potion into his mouth, and after a while, he woke up.

After drinking the magic potion, the king, Thorgar, Fenris, and Skrymir found a quiet spot in the forest where they could rest and reflect on their experiences. They settled down at the foot of a large tree and let the peace and tranquility of the forest's deep rustle fill their minds.

"Do you feel better now?" Skrymir asked, looking at his companions with care in his eyes.

Thorgar nodded slowly. "Yes, I feel much better. That drink is truly magical," he replied with a smile. "I can feel the energy flowing back into my veins."

Fenris, still young and full of curiosity, looked at his travel companion and added: "I am very impressed with the drink, had we just used it during the fight, we would have won."

I didn't think of that, said Skrymir, they came so suddenly. You couldn't know, said the king, I don't even know how they found the tree. They have been looking for the tree for hundreds of years, so it was very unfortunate that it was today they found it.

How do we get to Asgard now, asked Fenris with despair in his voice. There are no more apples left on the tree.

The sprite king, with a serious expression on his face, approached them. He carried a small envelope of leaves.

"Skrymir," the king began, his voice deep and resonant, "I know that you and your companions have faced great dangers to help us. As a thank you for your courage and bravery, I would like to give you the last apple, which I originally intended to give to the queen."

He opened the envelope and took the last apple, shining like the sun, in his hands. With a dignified gesture, he held it out to Skrymir. "Take this apple, and let it be a symbol of our gratitude and friendship."

Skrymir took the apple with respect and gratitude. He knew that this apple not only represented the sprite king's thanks but also a deep connection and trust between them.

"We are honored by your generosity, king," said Skrymir with sincerity. "We will carry this apple with us as a sign of our friendship."

After the intense battle and the rescue of the sprite king, Skrymir, Thorgar, and Fenris were welcomed to a magnificent dinner in honor of their heroic actions. The magical atmosphere in the sprite town was marked by joy and gratitude.

They were led into a large banquet hall, illuminated by glowing lanterns and filled with the scent of delicious dishes. The table was covered with a lavish banquet of the sprites' finest food and drink, and at the end of the table sat the sprite king, with a smile. "Welcome, my honored guests," declared the Wight King, his voice filled with gratitude. "I am deeply moved by your bravery and the unparalleled effort you have shown for our kingdom. Let us celebrate this joyous day and the friendship that has been forged between our peoples."

Skrymir, Thorgar, and Fenris were seated next to the king, showered with gifts and compliments. They enjoyed the lavish banquet and shared stories of their adventures with the curious wights, who listened attentively to every word.

During the dinner, promises of friendship and cooperation between humans and wights were exchanged, and festive tunes filled the room with joy and optimism for the future.

As the dinner drew to a close, the Wight King rose from his throne and lifted his goblet in a toast to their honored guests. "To our friends, who have proven themselves true heroes," he declared proudly. "May our friendship last forever, and may we always stand together against any threat that may come our way."

He then turned to the rest of the people.

"Dear friends, honored guests, and my beloved people,

"Today, we gather not only to celebrate our survival and our new friendship but also to reflect on the challenges we face. As you know, our valley has been blessed with magical apples that have been the source of our strength, our vitality, and our eternal youth. These apples have been our lifeblood, our connection to nature, and our hope for the future."

"But today, dear friends, we are forced to confront a harsh truth. The apples, our beloved apples, are no longer with us. They have been taken from us, and we now face the consequences of their loss. Without the apples, our land will decay, our magic will fade, and our people will suffer."

"I fear that if we do not find a solution, our wight race will be threatened with extinction. Without the power the apples gave us, we will lose our ability to sustain our lives and our community. We will lose our connection to our roots and our heritage. And although we will still be here, we will no longer be the same."

"Therefore, dear friends, it is crucial that we work together, that we unite our forces and our will to restore what we have lost. We must seek new paths, new opportunities, and never lose faith in our ability to overcome even the greatest challenges."

"Let us remember the magic of the apples, let us recall their significance, and let us act with courage and determination. Let us seek a new path that will lead us back to our former glory, and let us never forget that we are stronger together than apart."

"Thank you, my friends, for being here today. Let us move forward with hope in our hearts and courage in our souls. Let us together find the way back to the light, to strength, and to the blessing of the apple tree."

"For the future of the wights, for our future, let us stand together and fight. Thank you."

Skrymir looked over at Fenris, who lay on a blanket at the end of their table, with a lump in his throat. If only I had fought harder, Skrymir thought to himself.

As the party began, the great hall filled with life and laughter. Light from the sparkling crystal chandeliers cast shimmering reflections over the polished wooden tables, covered with the finest china and most delicate dishes. The aromas of culinary delights filled the air, from roasted meats to fresh vegetables and sweet desserts.

In the center of the table stood a magnificent bowl filled with juicy fruits and berries, and next to it, a splendid pitcher of golden drink. People from all corners of the wight world gathered, happy and festive, ready to celebrate and forget their sorrows for a while.

As the party was in full swing, a little wight sat down next to Skrymir. With a smile on his thin face, he offered a bowl to the giant. "Would you like to try a bite of this porridge? It's something I brought from the human world. Humans call it rice pudding," said the wight, winking slyly at Skrymir.

Skrymir, who had never tasted rice pudding before, looked curiously down at the steaming bowl. "Rice pudding?" he repeated, letting a large finger touch the white mass. It was warm and soft. "Why not? Let's give it a try."

With a large spoon, Skrymir took a mouthful of the creamy porridge. The taste of sweetness and spices filled his mouth, and he couldn't help but smile. "This is actually quite good!" he exclaimed, surprised.

The wight laughed and nodded. "Yes, it's one of the humans' delicacies. They especially eat it in the winter as a tradition." "Some people leave a bowl up for the mice in the attic, that's where I got it from," said the wight, laughing. "If you come again one day, you should try something called 'peppernuts.'" Skrymir nodded with a smile.

"Thorgar, Fenris, you should try this porridge," Skrymir called to them. "No, you don't become big and mighty by eating human food," Thorgar exclaimed.

As Skrymir continued to enjoy the rice pudding, more wights gathered around him, curious to try this delicacy. Soon, there was a whole group sharing stories about the human world and their own experiences.

Skrymir enjoyed the moment, the sense of community, and the warmth that the rice pudding brought. He realized that although there were many differences between wights, giants, and humans, there was also much they could learn from each other and share.

As the night progressed, the party only became more lively, filled with laughter, singing, and stories. And in the midst of it all sat Skrymir, with the wights, enjoying the moment and grateful for the new experience and the new friendship he had found that evening.

The king sat with the queen at the end of the table, with a smile on his face and a twinkle in his eye, grateful for everyone who had come to support the party and gather in the spirit of community. He raised his mug and toasted to a future filled with hope and magic, a life the wights hopefully would grow stronger than ever before.

The music began to play, and people started to dance, a feeling of unity and joy spread through the room. Everyone was united in the magic of the party, united in their desire to celebrate, to be together, and to fight for a better future.

The door burst open and in came large wooden trays with mead, not just ordinary mead; it was a special brew made from the finest berries gathered around the forest, carefully selected by the wights themselves for their magical properties and sweet taste.

Skrymir took a sip of the golden drink and immediately felt the magic of the berries dance on his tongue. It was a blend of sweetness and a deep, complex flavor that made one think of the deep forests from which the berries came.

Next to him sat a wight, whose face lit up with excitement. "Have you ever tasted anything so wonderful, Skrymir?" asked the wight with a twinkle in his eye.

Skrymir nodded, "Never. This is truly a drink for the gods."

The wight laughed, "That's what everyone says who tries our mead. The berries are harvested with great care and love. They bring happiness and joy to those who drink it."

During the party, the mead was shared around, and everyone enjoyed the lovely drink. It filled the air with a pleasant scent and created an atmosphere of festivity and renewed energy among the guests.

After a while, the Wight King stood up and gave a speech to thank Skrymir and his companions for their courage and help. "Tonight, we celebrate not only our friendship and our victory," he said, "but also the magic and beauty that our forests and berries bring to our world."

It was a night of joy, of community, and of hope. A night when the wights forgot their worries and celebrated life in all its splendor and beauty. A night that reminded them of the importance of standing together, of caring for each other, and of holding on to hope, even when darkness threatens.

Chapter 6: The Old Lady

The next morning, Skrymir, Thorgar, and Fenris awoke to the sound of birdsong and the first rays of the sun casting a soft light into the large cave. The joy of the feast and the magic of the mead had filled the air with warmth and satisfaction.

The Vætte King greeted them at the entrance to the valley where they had spent the night. His face wore a smile of gratitude and friendship. "Your visit has been an unforgettable event for us all," he said in a deep voice. "We will never forget the help you have provided us and the celebration we shared."

Skrymir extended his hand to give the Vætte King a firm handshake. "It was our honor to assist," he replied. "We are glad to have been of help and to enjoy your hospitality."

Thorgar and Fenris nodded in agreement, their faces lit by the morning light playing in their eyes. "Farewell, noble Vætir ," said Thorgar. "May your valley remain lush and peaceful."

Fenris wagged his tail and blew a gentle breeze towards the Vætir as a final goodbye. "May we meet again one day," he said with a deep, rumbling voice that carried a tone of gratitude and friendship.

The Vætte King waved them goodbye as they left the valley and headed back towards the world of humans. With each step, they carried the memories of their adventure in the world of the Vætir , and a new chapter of their journey awaited them.

With the apple safely in their possession and grateful hearts, Skrymir, Thorgar, and Fenris stepped out of the Vætir 's valley and into the deep forest. The sunlight still filtered through the leaves of the trees, creating a play of shadows and sunbeams on the forest floor.

Skrymir led the way, his long strides guiding them through the dense layer of fallen leaves and twigs. He reflected on their adventure, the Vætir they had met, and the wisdom they had shared.

Thorgar walked by his side, his eyes scanning the forest as if searching for something or someone. "We are approaching the border of my kingdom," he said thoughtfully. "Perhaps you would like to visit."

Fenris, eager as ever, sniffed the air and caught the scents of the forest - earth, moss, and the distant rustling of a stream. He turned to Skrymir with a twinkle in his eye. "Shall we visit?"

Skrymir smiled down at him. "We definitely should visit him, but first, we must pass by the old lady."

As they approached the edge of the forest, Fenris and Skrymir stopped. Thorgar looked at them questioningly, his eyes filled with wonder and a hint of sadness. "We would like to say goodbye here," began Skrymir, patting Fenris on the shoulder.

Fenris nodded and smiled up at Thorgar. "It has been an honor to travel with you, Thorgar. We will visit soon."

Thorgar nodded back and extended his hand. "Thank you for everything, friends. Take care out there." The two parted with a firm handshake before Thorgar continued his way out of the forest.

Fenris and Skrymir turned towards the deeper part of the forest, where the old lady's dwelling awaited. The sun began to sink lower in the sky, and the forest shadows grew longer and darker. With each step, the air thickened with mystique and anticipation.

Deep in the forest, where the trees stood tall and dense, and secrets lurked in the shadows, sunlight pierced the thick foliage, casting patches of light on the soft forest floor.

After hours of walking, Skrymir noticed a large, angular rock a little further ahead. It looked like an ordinary rock from a distance, but as they got closer, they realized it was not a rock at all.

"Look here, Skrymir," said Fenris, pointing with his snout. "This is no ordinary rock."

Before Fenris could say more, Skrymir approached and knocked on the rock with a stick. The rock shook slightly and began to slowly roll aside, revealing eyes and a large mouth. It was a troll, and it did not look pleased.

"Forgive us," said Skrymir, "We didn't think anyone lived here."

The troll looked at them skeptically, its eyes shining in the dim light. "No one has disturbed me in thousands of years," said the troll with a deep, resonant voice. "What brings you here?"

Skrymir stepped forward. "We are looking for an old lady," he said cautiously. "We do not wish to disturb anyone; we just want to find the lady. Can you help us?"

The troll laughed mockingly. "An old lady? Why should I help you?"

Skrymir took a deep breath and said, "We need the lady to reach Asgard. Without her, Jotunheim will lose a vital part of its magic."

The troll's eyes softened slightly. "If what you say is true, I cannot refuse help. But first, you must prove that you are worthy. Only the brave and cunning deserve assistance."

The troll, with its rough, gray skin and large, knotted nose, stepped forward from the stone. "Hmm, what shall we think of?" it grumbled.

Skrymir stepped forward, "Now, nothing that takes too long."

The troll snorted, "To prove your strength and worthiness, you must first pass my test of strength."

Fenris stepped forward, eager to demonstrate his strength. "We are ready," he said.

The troll smiled, a wicked smile, and pointed to a large, heavy stone next to it. "Lift this stone and throw it overhead. Only then will you have proven that you are worthy."

Skrymir looked at the stone, which seemed enormous and insurmountable. He took a deep breath and grabbed the stone with both hands. With a great effort, he lifted it and threw it high into the air. The stone flew through the air and landed directly on top of the troll with a loud crash.

Fenris watched in amazement as Skrymir shrugged. "That was not intentional," he said.

The troll was now more than just impressed; it had been completely buried under the stone. "That was... impressive," a voice mumbled faintly from under the stone, pointing in the direction of the old lady's house.

Fenris and Skrymir looked at each other and then at the buried troll. "We better continue our journey," said Skrymir cautiously. "Thank you for your test."

The troll nodded weakly, still buried. "Go now in peace. May your journey be joyful and your errands generous. But beware, the old lady is not as she appears."

With the troll's words, Skrymir and Fenris continued their journey, ready to meet the old lady and complete their mission. After a while, they came to a clearing where a small, old cottage stood.

Around the cottage was a garden filled with herbs and plants, and a fire was lit in front of the entrance. The old lady sat there, just as they had left her, but her eyes lit up when she saw them coming.

"Welcome back, my friends," she said with a warm voice. "I knew you would come back."

Fenris wagged his tail and walked up to her, while Skrymir approached with a smile. "We have been looking forward to this," he said. "Now you will hear a good story."

With a twinkling glint in her eye, the old lady invited them into her cottage, ready to share another evening of stories, wisdom, and friendship.

Skrymir and Fenris stepped into the cottage, a cozy and rustic cabin with thick wooden beams that smelled of resin and a thatched roof. The interior of the cottage was illuminated by a soft, golden glow from the fireplace, which crackled cheerily at one end of the room.

Fenris immediately went to the fireplace, whose warm rays were attractive after walking through the cool forest. He lay down comfortably in front of the flames, which danced hypnotically in the fire.

Skrymir took a seat on a sturdy wooden chair next to him and began to tell of their adventures in the world of the Vætir. He described the breathtaking valley and the magical apple tree, the friendly Vætte King, and the terrible fate that threatened the Vætir due to the lack of apples.

As he spoke, Fenris listened attentively, his eyes resting on the flames that cast long shadows on the walls of the cottage. He nodded occasionally, especially when Skrymir mentioned their trials and triumphs, as if he were already dreaming of the next adventures.

The old lady, with her wrinkled face and deep, serious eyes, listened intently to Skrymir's and Fenris' stories. But when they reached the point about the surprising attack from Brage and Idun, she could feel the anger bubbling inside her like a boiling pot.

She straightened up in her chair, and her gaze became sharp as steel. "You should have used the potion," she said with a sharp voice that cut through the room like a cold wind. "It was given to you for a reason."

Skrymir looked up, his eyes filled with apology. "We did not know there would be an attack," he explained. "We thought we could manage without it."

The old lady sighed deeply, and her facial expression softened slightly, but still with an undertone of concern. "The potion is not only for healing physical wounds but also for protecting you from the unexpected," she said. "You must always be prepared for the unforeseen, especially when you embark on dangerous adventures."

Fenris looked down, somewhat embarrassed by their mistake, while Skrymir nodded and took the lady's words to heart. "We thank you for your teaching," he said humbly. "However, they did not get all the apples, we got one from the king."

The old lady's face softened even more, and she nodded with a smile. "What," she said. "Did you get an apple from the king?" Yes, Skrymir replied, and took out the apple.

With a sudden smile that lit up her wrinkled face like the sun breaking through the clouds, the old lady reached out and gently took the one apple Skrymir and Fenris had brought. She lifted it up, examined its glowing skin and the deep, rich color that told of its magical interior.

"An apple from the Vætir ," she murmured softly, "Such I have not seen in many years."

She let her fingers glide over the smooth skin and took a deep breath, as if she were absorbing its essence. Then she looked at Skrymir and Fenris with a warm smile. "This apple brings back memories of old days and joyful times. "Thank you, my friends."

Skrymir and Fenris exchanged a look of relief and joy. They had been unsure how the old lady would react, but her joy was evident. It was as if the apple had opened a window to her past, and they were glad to have been able to bring her this joy.

"It is a gift from us," said Fenris proudly, "a sign of our friendship and your guidance."

The old lady nodded with a crooked smile. "I will appreciate it," she said, "I will appreciate it."

The evening passed, and the stars began to twinkle in the sky through the small windows in the walls of the cottage. In the golden glow from the fireplace, the two friends continued to share their stories, bound together by the adventure and the warmth of the flames.

With a smile almost as radiant as the apple's skin, Skrymir said, "The Vætir 's mead was the most enchanting I have ever tasted. "A true delicacy for the soul."

The old lady nodded, and with a smile that revealed a secretive joy, she fetched a shiny jar from a shelf next to the fireplace. The jar was decorated with ancient runes and patterns that told of past glories.

"I am glad to hear that you like mead," she said. With an elegant motion, she opened the jar and poured a golden liquid into a ceramic mug. The mead shimmered in the light from the fire, its scent filling the air with a sweet and enchanting aroma.

"Try this," she said, handing the mug to Skrymir.

He carefully took the mug, took a deep breath, and let his nose absorb the fragrance. Then he took a small sip. The taste of the mead was nothing short of enchanting. It was sweet, but not too sweet, with a subtle floral undertone and a depth that revealed layers of complex flavors.

Skrymir let the mead swirl around in his mouth, enjoying every second before looking up at the old lady with a satisfied smile. "This is truly a nectar of the gods," he said with reverence in his voice.

The old lady nodded contentedly. "It is a recipe that has been passed down for generations," she said. "I am glad you liked it." "It is a gift from me to you, as thanks for everything you have done for me."
Fenris, with a spark of curiosity in his eyes, turned to the old woman. "What do you actually need the apple for?" he asked, his ears perked up in anticipation of a new adventure.

The old woman smiled warmly and settled into her creaky armchair. "To tell you the truth, my young friend," she began, "I've been given a potion by an ancient elf. It's a concoction that allows even an old lady like me to rival the greatest gods."

She took a deep breath and continued with a crooked smile, "The only thing missing to complete the potion was an apple from the spirits' tree. It's the magic of the apple that gives the potion its full power and makes it invincible."

Fenris nodded in understanding. "So that's why you were so worried about the apple," he said, realizing its importance. "It's incredible to think how such a small apple can be so significant."

The old woman smiled and gently patted Fenris on the head. "Yes, my boy. It's the magic of the little things in life that often have the greatest impact."

"Now that you've helped me so much, I think you should see what it can do," the old woman said, fetching an old glass bottle filled with golden liquid. She carefully placed the shiny, red spirit apple into the golden potion. As the apple touched the liquid, it briefly bubbled, and a faint glow spread through the potion.

"Watch something magical," the old woman said with a sly smile. She gently stirred the mixture with her long, curled finger, covered in wrinkles and age spots. The potion changed color from golden to a deep, ruby red, while a scent of freshness and energy filled the room.

Skrymir, Fenris, and the old woman intensely watched the mixture as it began to fizz and foam. After a moment, they saw the apple dissolve completely into the potion.

"This mixture will enhance its power," the old woman explained. "Now, it can truly work wonders. Try a small sip, but just a tiny one."

Skrymir carefully took the bottle of enchanted liquid from the old woman, his hands trembling slightly with excitement. "This is incredible," he murmured as he brought the bottle to his lips and took a small sip.

Fenris, who had been sitting patiently by the side, curiously stared at the bottle. He took it from Skrymir and drank a gulp. A renewed energy flowed through him, and his eyes lit up with newfound strength.

"Now we're ready," Skrymir declared confidently. "Wow, I feel like I could lift the whole of Jotunheim," he exclaimed.

The old woman nodded with a crooked smile, her eyes twinkling with gratitude. "Yes, just wait and see."

Hours passed, and the bottle of mead was nearly empty. The old woman, half-asleep, mumbled about the old times in Jotunheim.

The old woman affectionately smiled at Fenris's curious eyes. "I'm more into riddles and magic than potions," she said in a dreamy voice. "But I have a riddle so puzzling that no one has yet solved it."

Skrymir and Fenris exchanged a look of excitement and challenge. "If we solve your riddle," Skrymir proposed, "will you give us more of your potion?"

The old woman chuckled softly and nodded. "Yes, if you can solve my riddle, you may have half of the potion."

Fenris's tail wagged eagerly, and he stepped closer. "Let's hear it, and we'll find the answer."

The old woman clapped her hands, causing a gentle wind to blow through the small room. "Listen carefully," she said. "I can be as light as a feather, but even the strongest man cannot hold me for more than a few minutes. What am I?"

Skrymir and Fenris stared intently at the old woman, trying to decipher the deeper meaning of the riddle. They quietly muttered to themselves, attempting to figure it out.

After a few moments of silence, Fenris's eyes brightened with understanding. "It must be a breath," he said proudly. "For a breath can be as light as a feather and cannot be held by anyone for more than a few minutes."

The old woman clapped her hands enthusiastically. "Correct, my friend! You've solved my riddle, and I'll keep my promise." She reached under the table, pulled out a bottle, and filled it with the shimmering, golden liquid.

Skrymir took the bottle carefully, his eyes gleaming with gratitude. "Thank you, venerable lady. We will appreciate your generosity and use this elixir wisely."

The old woman smiled crookedly, pleased with how happy Skrymir and Fenris were to have solved her riddle. But in her eyes, there was a hint of a new challenge. "Well, you've guessed the first one, but let's see if you can solve another," she said with a hint of teasing in her voice. "If you win, you get the rest of the potion. But if you lose, the potion comes back to me, and you owe me a favor."

Skrymir and Fenris exchanged a look of excitement and challenge. They both nodded eagerly, ready to take on the new challenge.

The old woman clapped her hands and began the riddle. "I have a key but no lock. I have space but no rooms. You can enter me, but you can never leave. What am I?"

Skrymir and Fenris thought hard, trying to find the answer. They quietly muttered to themselves, trying to figure it out.

After a few minutes of silence, Fenris's eyes lit up with understanding. "It must be a map," he said triumphantly. "For a map has a key for symbols, it holds spaces of places, and once you're in its depiction, you're captured in its scope."

The old woman looked a bit surprised but quickly returned to a smile. "You're right, my young friend," she said with a slight sigh of irritation. "You are quite good at these riddles." "Here's the potion, as promised."

With a small sigh of resignation, the old woman handed the bottle to Skrymir, who accepted it with a grateful smile. "Thank you, venerable lady. We will use this potion wisely and appreciate your generosity."

The old woman nodded, still slightly annoyed but also impressed by Skrymir and Fenris's riddle-solving skills. "Take care with the potion in the great forests," she warned, "many will be after it, so be careful."

The old woman looked at them with a twinkle in her eye, her wrinkled face set in a warm smile. "Now that you have my potion, you'd better be on your way before I change my mind and keep it for myself," she said with a laugh in her voice.

Skrymir and Fenris chuckled lightly and thanked her again for her generosity. "We will heed your warning and be on our guard," Skrymir said, holding the potion bottle in his hand.

"Yes, thank you for the riddles and your generosity," Fenris added with a smile. "We hope to meet again."

The old woman looked deeply into their eyes, her gaze now softer. "Before you go," she began, "I promised to tell you how to find Odin. There's an old sage here in the forest, one who knows Odin's hidden places. He can lead you to him."

Skrymir and Fenris looked at her in surprise. "Can you tell us where we can find this sage?" Fenris asked curiously.

"Yes," the old woman replied, "He lives in an old tower that rises above the treetops. It's a long journey from here, but if you follow this path," she pointed to a narrow trail leading into the forest, "it will lead you straight to him."

"We thank you," Skrymir said with deep gratitude in his voice. "Your advice and gifts will not be forgotten." "We will follow the path and seek this sage so he can show us the way to Odin."

"Be on your guard," the old woman cautioned. "The road is filled with dangers and challenges. But you have already proven yourselves brave and wise. I believe you will find what you seek. And take care of the potion; it must not fall into the wrong hands."

With a final nod and a wave goodbye from the old woman, Skrymir and Fenris set off on the narrow path leading into the heart of the forest. As they walked, they pondered what lay ahead and how this new information would alter the course of their adventure.

With the forest around them, the song of birds as background music, and a new goal in sight, they continued their journey, hopeful and resolute in their quest to find Odin.

Chapter 7: The Road to Thorgar's Realm

In the deep twilight, with the dense forest trees casting long shadows, Skrymir and Fenris walk through the dark woods of Jotunheim. The sound of their footsteps is muffled by the thick foliage beneath them, as the nocturnal animals begin their chorus.

Fenris looks up at Skrymir and suggests, "What if we visit Thorgar, the giant king? His castle is right on our way."

Skrymir pauses to think, then nods in agreement, "Yes, that might be a good idea. He could help us find the path we're seeking."

They delve deeper into the forest where the trees stand close together, and the sun's rays barely touch the ground through the dense branches. Suddenly, they encounter a mysterious creature. It has shiny, raven-colored feathers that change hue with its movements. Its eyes are deep and sparkle like the stars on a clear night.

Skrymir and Fenris stop and cautiously observe the creature. It moves gracefully between the trees, almost as if dancing through the forest.

"Good day," the creature says with a voice that sounds like the wind rustling through the leaves. "What brings you to my part of the forest?"

Stepping forward, Skrymir replies, "We are on our way to meet Thorgar, the giant king. Do you know the way?"

The creature smiles, its feathers shimmering in the faint sunlight. "Ah, Thorgar, the giant king is known to all beings in the forest. But the way is not easy. You must follow the path that leads through the old oak trees, then turn north at the large rock formation."

Fenris growls softly, "Thank you for the information. Who are you?"

The creature nods and responds, "I am Lyrna, the guardian of the forest. I watch over those who wander through this forest and protect its secrets."

Thorgar studies Lyrna and asks, "You seem to know many of the forest's secrets. Have you heard of any dangers on our path?"

Lyrna nods slowly, "The trees speak of a figure seeking you. Be cautious as you approach Thorgar's realm."

With that advice, they continue their journey, grateful for Lyrna's guidance. The forest around them now seems both more inviting and mysterious, and they proceed with caution and excitement in their hearts.

As they move through the forest, Fenris suddenly senses a strange change in the atmosphere around them. He stops abruptly and lifts his nose, as if trying to detect a distant scent. "Do you feel that?" he asks, peering into the dense foliage.

Skrymir looks at him quizzically. "What do you mean, Fenris?" he asks, beginning to feel uneasy.

Fenris' eyes search through the forest's dark shadows. "It feels like we are being watched. As if someone or something is keeping an eye on us," he says, frowning deeply.

Thorgar grabs a large stone and says, "We must be on guard. This forest is full of secrets, and not all are friendly."

Suddenly, a faint but eerie sound breaks the silence. It sounds like a whisper coming from all directions at once. "Who dares to enter my forest?"

They quickly turn around, trying to locate the source of the voice. But the forest is dense and impenetrable, and all they can see are the dark tree trunks and the gentle shadows dancing between them.

"We are friends of the forest," Fenris shouts into the air. "We are merely seeking Thorgar, the giant king."

After a brief pause, the voice responds again, this time softer but still filled with mistrust. "Thorgar, you say? Why do you seek him?"

Fenris steps forward and says, "We are just visiting an old friend."

There is a long silence, and the three can feel the forest waiting for something. Finally, the mysterious voice says, "Follow the path to the right, to the old oak trees. There you will find Thorgar's realm. But be careful, for the forest has many eyes and ears."

"Thank you," shouts Skrymir.

As they followed the trail, the surroundings began to change, and they realized they might have taken the wrong path. "This doesn't look right," Skrymir exclaimed.

Suddenly, from the bushes beside the path, a giant serpent slithered out. Its scales glittered in the faint light filtering through the trees, and its eyes shone with a glowing intensity.

Fenris abruptly stopped, his senses heightened. He sensed the serpent -like presence before it appeared, and his fur bristled. Skrymir pulled back his muscular arms, ready to attack.

The serpent moved towards them, its body long and supple, its tongue as sharp as a knife. It hissed softly, warning them to turn back, but its movements showed no sign of aggression. Instead, it seemed to be guarding the path like a watchdog.

Driven by curiosity, Fenris slowly approached, his eyes fixed on the serpent . He could sense there was more to this creature than its fearsome appearance.

The serpent raised its head and whispered, almost hissing, "I only want the potion you carry. If you give it to me, no harm will come to you."

However, Fenris, on guard, whispered to Skrymir that they had promised the old lady not to lose the potion. He shook his head firmly and said, "We cannot give you the potion. We promised to protect it."

The serpent 's eyes sharpened, and its body tensed like a spring ready to strike. "So you want a fight," it hissed.

The serpent lunged at them with incredible speed, its shiny scales reflecting the sunlight from above, giving it an almost eerie glow. Fenris and Skrymir tried to fend off the attack, but the serpent 's speed and strength were overwhelming.

They dodged its bites and strikes swiftly, but it was clear they were being overpowered. Fenris growled and tried to bite into the serpent 's body, but it seemed nearly impossible to hit the swift creature.

After several intense minutes of fighting, it became clear they were losing. Skrymir shouted, "We need to escape!" He grabbed Fenris by the collar and pulled him along as they began to run through the forest, away from the dangerous serpent.

The serpent roared angrily and tried to follow them, but its large body made it slower, and it couldn't keep up with their rapid escape through the dense trees and bushes.

They ran as fast as they could until they were sure they had distanced themselves enough from the serpent. They reached a clearing and thought they were safe, but as they approached, they could hear the sound of rushing water.

They reached the clearing and found themselves by the mighty river Elivågen, which wound through Jotunheim. Standing on the riverbank, Skrymir looked at Fenris. "I never learned to swim," Fenris dipped his paw in the water, "Never swam before."

Skrymir took out the bottles of potion, "Let's follow the old lady's advice and use the potion she gave us this time." They both took a sip from the bottle and immediately felt a surge of energy.

Suddenly, a serpent's head peeked out from the dense forest, glaring angrily at Skrymir and Fenris. "Have you drunk my potion?" the serpent exclaimed. It rose up, doubling in size compared to Skrymir, and hissed, "Then I must kill you before you drink it all," and attacked.

The serpent advanced with a menacing look, its shiny scales dangerously glinting in the sunlight. Fenris and Skrymir stood ready, their gazes focused and determined. With a roar, Fenris leaped forward, his teeth bared menacingly. Skrymir quickly followed, his massive arm stretched out to grab the serpent's body.

Their attack was coordinated and powerful, but the serpent was a formidable opponent. It used its speed to dodge their attacks while wrapping around them in an attempt to capture them in its grip.

This time, however, the fight was different. Thanks to the potion, both Skrymir and Fenris felt an unmatched strength and speed. They were now equal opponents for the cunning serpent.

In the heat of battle, the serpent devised a cunning plan. With a sudden magical burst, it sent a powerful gust of wind towards Fenris, causing him to stagger backward. Before the two could react, the serpent used its magic to send Fenris flying over the bank of the river Elivågen, where he landed with a splash.

Skrymir watched in shock as Fenris struggled to swim against the current and get back on land. The serpent 's head turned triumphantly towards Skrymir, ready to continue the fight, now with an upper hand.

Skrymir grabbed a log from the bank, standing alone but still strong and unyielding on the bank of Elivågen, his powerful hands embracing the massive log. His eyes were locked on the serpent , ready for round two of the fight.

The serpent slithered with superiority, its shiny eyes fixed on Skrymir. "Now I'll kill you!" it hissed, with a venomous smile around its sharp teeth.

Just at that moment, a dark shadow cut through the water in the river. A large, dark figure appeared in the water. It was Midgard , now risen to help his friends.

Midgard lifted itself from the river's depths, dramatically parting the water as its enormous body broke the surface. Water droplets sparkled like thousands of tiny diamonds. Midgard , whose scales were like armored plates, shone with a supernatural sheen.

Opposite Midgard , almost as impressive, was his opponent. The other serpent was covered in darker scales that seemed to absorb the light around it, giving it a more menacing look. Its eyes were like glowing coals, and each movement left a faint, eerie hiss in the air.

The serpent , with its shiny scales and venomous gaze, slithered towards Skrymir with quick and relentless movements. Skrymir, however, was not to be outdone. With the log, he defended himself against the serpent , parrying its attacks and striking back with powerful blows.

Midgard , with its gigantic serpent body, came to the rescue. As their battle began, the two titans rushed through the forest, breaking trees and crushing the undergrowth under their weight. Midgard took the initiative, its head shooting forward like an arrow from a bow, trying to catch its foe in a deadly bite. The opponent, however, was lightning-fast and twisted away at the last moment, sending Midgard crashing into a massive oak that creaked dangerously under the impact.

The serpent s' movements created a symphony of destruction; each time they coiled around each other, there was a terrifying creaking and cracking from trees and earth being torn up. They fought for dominance, each trying to strangle and overpower the other with their powerful bodies. Midgard used its size to try to squeeze the life out of its opponent, who with desperate and wild strength burst free time and again.

The air was filled with their hissing and roaring, and the forest seemed to shake with each contact.

After an intense duel, where the ground shook under their trampling, and the forest echoed with roars and hisses, the serpent began to show signs of weakness. It lost its strength, its movements became sluggish, and its attacks less coordinated.

With a final powerful swing from Skrymir's log and a tightening from Midgard , the serpent was overpowered. With a loud hiss and a last desperate attempt to fight back, it was pushed back and sent fleeing into the dark forest.

Skrymir and Midgard stood back, tired but triumphant, their allied strength and cooperation had prevailed over the dreaded serpent . They exchanged a look of recognition, affirming their teamwork and skills, before Midgard pulled Fenris out of the water for the second time.

Fenris shook himself, while Skrymir covered his face with a smile.

Relieved after the intense battle, they were happy to be together again, united in their common goal. Midgard , with its shiny scales and impressive size, glistened in the sun as it looked gratefully at the other two.

"It was lucky you dipped your paws, Fenris, and that you don't wash them," Midgard laughed. "I could smell you from the other end of Elivågen." Fenris looked up with a smile and laughed.

Skrymir took out the bottle of potion and offered Midgard a sip. Midgard looked at them with grateful eyes, rolled slightly to drink, and immediately felt a power surge through him.

"I really shouldn't drink more potion," said Midgard. "Why not?" Fenris asked curiously. "It seems I keep growing since I drank the last potion. If it continues, I won't fit in the river anymore," Midgard said with a laugh.

Fenris laughed, wagged his tail, and lightly jumped around, full of life and energy, ready for the adventures ahead. The three friends looked at each other with a gaze that said more than a thousand words—a look of mutual respect, trust, and everlasting friendship.

"We will visit the Giant King Thorgar," said Skrymir. "Do you know if Elivågen can take us there?" "I believe so," said Midgard. "I can give you a lift part of the way." The two thanked him for his help. "Just hop on my back, and we'll swim along Elivågen." His words carried a calm authority that reassured the other two.

Skrymir and Fenris exchanged a look filled with trust and consent. Skrymir, with his massive stature, climbed first onto Midgard's shiny back and stretched a hand down to help Fenris up. Fenris jumped up, landing lightly between Midgard's scales and positioned himself close to Skrymir.

With a powerful tail swipe, Midgard pushed himself out into Elivågen. The water around them splashed and bubbled, but Midgard swam with a strength and elegance that surprised them.

As they glided through the deep water, they passed forests, mountains, and open plains. The landscape was marked by majestic mountains, whose peaks reached up to the sky like the arms of frozen titans. Deep, mysterious forests stretched as far as the eye could see, where the old trunks of trees whispered secrets of the past. Hidden valleys, lush and green, protected by high cliffs, lay between these titanic trees. Throughout Jotunheim, there were bubbling rivers and waterfalls that danced down the cliffs with an almost deafening roar. Despite its wild and untamed nature, there was an undeniable beauty and peace over this land, starkly contrasting the raw and brutal figures it housed.

As they swam through the deep, blue waters of Elivågen, a wonderful underwater world opened up to them. Fish of all the colors of the rainbow swam around them, and the sunlight created dancing rays on the ocean floor.

Midgard pointed with his large head down towards the enchanting world below them. "Here," he said in a deep voice, "live the sea folk. Nixies and nymphs, mermaids, and other magical Vættir ."

Fenris looked fascinated down through the clear water. "Are they friendly?"

Midgard smiled. "Some are friendly, others are more shy. But most will leave us alone if we don't disturb them."

Midgard continued on his way, and the three friends followed him, enjoying the sight of the underwater world's beauty. After a while, Skrymir said, "It's incredible. I've never seen anything like it."

"It's a world of its own," said Fenris dreamily. "Imagine if we could visit it one day."

Midgard nodded. "Maybe one day. But now we need to continue to the land of the giant king."

As Midgard swam with his two friends on his back, they began to share their experiences from the realm of the water spirits. Skrymir told with a smile about the beautiful feast and the enchanting rice pudding they had tasted.

"Rice pudding from Midgard is something special," said Fenris with a twinkle in his eye. "It was a flavor I've never experienced before."

Midgard made a curious sound. "Rice pudding from Midgard , you say? That sounds like something I'd like to try."

Skrymir laughed. "I think you would like it. It's sweet and creamy, and it warms you up all the way inside."

Midgard sighed. "I'd like to try that, it's cold being in the water. I've always been curious about Midgard . I've heard so much about it but have never had the chance to visit the place."
Fenris patted Midgard on the head. "Maybe one day we can leave. But first, we need to save Jotunheim."

Midgard nodded. "Of course, I understand. But if you ever go to Midgard, will you promise to take me with you so I can have some rice pudding?"

Skrymir smiled broadly. "We promise."

They were now in the middle of the deep Elivågen, and as the foam splashed around them, suddenly three beautiful mermaids emerged from the deep waters. Their song filled the air with an enchanting melody that made even the old waves sound like a symphony.

Skrymir was almost hypnotized by the sight of the beautiful mermaids. His eyes were glued to them, and a smile played on his lips. "I think I'm in love," he murmured, dreamily watching the mermaids' dancing movements.

Fenris and Midgard couldn't help but laugh a little at their friend. "How can you fall in love with them? They have fish bodies underwater," Fenris said with a chuckle.

Skrymir shook his head and replied, "I can't explain it, there's just something about them." He continued to stare at the mermaids as they sang and danced around them.

The mermaids' song was both enchanting and soothing, but Fenris and Midgard couldn't help being a bit skeptical. They had heard stories about the mermaids' enchanting songs, which could lure sailors to get lost or even drown.

"You need to be careful, Skrymir," Fenris warned. "They might seduce you with their song and pull you home with them, and you can't breathe underwater."

But Skrymir was deeply captivated and couldn't help being a bit in love with the mermaids' beauty and song. "I don't think they mean any harm," he replied dreamily.

As the mermaids' song continued to resonate in the air, the water around them became clearer and clearer. The mermaids swam closer and looked curiously at the three friends. "Come with us," one mermaid sang enticingly. "We will show you the beauties beneath the sea's surface."

Fenris, Midgard, and Skrymir looked at each other, unsure whether to accept the mermaids' offer. But before they could respond, the largest mermaid dove down and touched Midgard with her glittering tail. Suddenly, they felt a change: they were pulled underwater and could now breathe beneath the surface.

Fenris laughed and swam around underwater. "This is fantastic," he thought.

Midgard, who still stayed close to the surface with his large body, rolled his eyes playfully. "Come on, this is a fantastic opportunity! Think of all the adventures I'm missing on land. I can't wait to show you experiences under the water."

Convinced by Midgard's curiosity and a bit excited about the adventure themselves, the three friends nodded to each other and swam down with the mermaids. They were immediately surrounded by colorful corals, mysterious caves, and schools of shimmering fish that danced around them like living stars.

The mermaids led them deeper and deeper, where the light from the surface almost disappeared, but the underwater world was even more enchanting. They swam through ancient abandoned cities where sea plants swayed in the gentle current, and mysterious Vættir peeked curiously at them from hidden caves.

As they continued swimming through the crystal-clear water, the outlines of a magnificent castle began to take shape before them. Towers and spires stretched upward like corals that had grown over millennia, and it all shimmered in countless shades of blue.

The mermaids sang an enchanting melody as they led them through the emerald gardens and into a portal that took them to the castle's grand hall. They stood there, completely wet but able to breathe normally, with no water inside the castle.

Here they were greeted by Rán, the goddess of the sea, who sat on a throne made of starfish and seashells. Rán's eyes were as deep as the ocean's depths, and her hair flowed around her like seaweed in the ocean's currents. "Welcome to my realm," she said with a voice that rumbled like distant thunder. "Who are you, and what brings you to my castle?"

When Rán saw the three mermaids without any treasure, her face darkened. Her eyes became sharp as icebergs, and her voice sounded sharp and cold.

"Mermaids," Rán began, "Where are your treasures? You know that everyone who comes to my castle must bring a treasure with them."

The mermaids' gaze fell to the sand as if they were ashamed. "We thought that our guests would be treasure enough for you, Rán," said the eldest mermaid cautiously.

Rán sighed deeply. "Mermaids, how many times must I say it? You know the rules. You must capture giants carrying something valuable and bring their treasure to me. Otherwise, you will never be allowed to leave my realm."

"Well, we'll have to make do, to the eternal treasure chamber with them," Rán exclaimed and snapped her fingers. They were sent there by a magical force they did not yet understand.

Chapter 8: The Infinite Treasury

They now stood among endless corridors within a gigantic treasury, overwhelmed by the sight. It was the largest they had ever seen. Gold, silver, gemstones, and treasures from distant lands gleamed and sparkled in the light.

There, in the eternal treasury, where glittering treasures and magical items filled the room, Midgard felt a heaviness in his soul. The great serpent regretted dragging his friends into what seemed to him a dull and seemingly hopeless adventure.

As they began walking up one of the corridors, Midgard turned cautiously to the group. "I'm really sorry," he began in a subdued voice that sounded like a low roar. "I thought this adventure would be exciting and adventurous, but it has turned out to be boring. Who knows how long we'll be stuck here."

Skrymir and Fenris stopped and looked at the large serpent, its scales sparkling and eyes enormous and sad.

"It's not your fault," Skrymir said gently. "We chose to come with the mermaids, and even though the adventure hasn't been very thrilling, we've seen new things and experienced being underwater."

Midgard smiled gratefully, touched by Skrymir's words. "Thanks for being such good friends; I'll find a way out of here."

While they were talking, Skrymir suddenly noticed something that caught his attention: an axe. It lay seemingly forgotten among the glittering treasures. But there was something about it that piqued his interest.

"Look here," Skrymir exclaimed, pointing at the axe. "This axe looks old, yet it has an aura of power and mystery. There are runes on it that I can't decipher. It must have a significance beyond the ordinary."

Fenris and Midgard stopped to look at the axe. It was made of shiny metal that gleamed in the dim light of the treasury. The notches along the blade spoke of many years of use and battle.

"Do you think this axe could help us escape this boring place?" Midgard asked, looking at Skrymir.

"I don't know," Skrymir replied, "but something inside me says I should take it with us."

Carefully, Skrymir took the axe and tied it to his belt. They then continued their journey through the treasury.

As they walked through the endless corridors filled with glittering riches, they suddenly encountered an ancient dwarf, a large bunch of keys dangling from his belt.

The dwarf stared in astonishment at our adventurers. "Well, well, well, what do we have here?" he muttered to himself, stroking his gray beard. "Living treasures, I haven't seen that in my many years as guardian of this treasury."

"I am the Treasure Keeper," said the dwarf with a deep nod. His face was angular and marked by countless years as guardian of the infinite treasury. His gray beard was wild, and his eyes carried the wisdom and experience of centuries of protecting the treasures.

"I was chosen by the ancient powers to guard this treasure and protect its riches," he continued. "As a dwarf of ancient heritage, I have dedicated my life to this task."

He pointed to the key bunch he wore by his side. "This is my symbol of authority and responsibility."

Midgard interrupts the treasure keeper, who is in the middle of introducing himself. "We don't have all day; we're looking for a way out," Midgard explains how they entered the treasury.

The treasure keeper listens attentively and nods understandingly. "Finding a way out of this labyrinthine place is no easy task," he says seriously. "It's an endless maze, and there are dangerous spirits at every corner. If you survive and find the exit, you'll meet Nøkken, who is chained to the exit, playing his harp so that all who come close are enchanted."

He shares his knowledge about the dungeon with them and points out some possible routes they could try. "Be careful, there are many dangers and pitfalls here," he warns. "But if you stick together and use your wit and courage, you might find a way to the exit."

Midgard , tired of the dwarf's monotonous talk, suddenly exclaims: "What? No great Vættir to fight? I can't take it anymore! This is too boring!"

Fenris and Skrymir look at each other, surprised to see the serpent 's usual calm broken by frustration.

Fenris, always the calm one of the group, takes a deep breath and says, "Calm down, Midgard . We'll find a way out of this."

But Midgard refuses to be reassured. "I want some of that magic potion you have," he insists.

Skrymir hesitates, worried about what the magic potion might do to Midgard 's already unstable mind. "Aren't you afraid of getting too big?" said Skrymir. "It's a risk I'm willing to take to get out of this boring place," Midgard exclaims.

Finally, convinced that it's the only thing that can bring some life back to Midgard 's mood, he gives him a little.

With a roar of new energy, Midgard shouts, "Hop on, now let's get out of here!" They jump onto his back and wave goodbye to the treasure keeper, who stands gaping.

Midgard winds his way through the labyrinth's corridors, crushing treasures, statues, and art with his powerful body. Skrymir and Fenris cling to his back, leading through the chaotic journey. Evil spirits try in vain to stop the great serpent , but they hardly get a swing before Midgard just winds through or over them.

Finally, after smashing their way through the last obstacles, they see a faint glow in the distance. It's the exit! Midgard accelerates, eager to get out of this claustrophobic labyrinth.

Midgard smashes through the last part of the labyrinth with Skrymir and Fenris clinging to his shiny scales. When they reach the exit, they stop abruptly, surprised by the sight in front of them.
In front of them stands an impressive metal gate, decorated with complex patterns and engravings.

At the top of the gate sits Nøkken, as the treasure keeper mentioned, with long wet hair falling over his shoulders, and his fingers elegantly dancing over the strings of his harp. The music fills the air, a mix of melancholy and mystique.

"Nøkken! It's an honor to meet you," says Skrymir with respect in his voice. "I've heard about your melodies that can seduce even the bravest souls."

Nøkken smiles faintly and stops playing. "Thank you," he says. "I have wandered this labyrinth for many years, played my melodies for those who came down here, and often warned them of the dangers in the labyrinth."

Fenris looks curiously at Nøkken. "Why are you sitting by this gate, Nøkken?"

Nøkken lowers his gaze, as if remembering old times. "Many years ago, my beloved was captured by Rán, and I was banished here because I tried to save her. I have often sat by this gate, hoping that someone would open it one day so I could run up and save her."

Fenris listened intently. "How can we help you, Nøkken?"

Nøkken looks up with tears in his eyes. "Can you help me get my beloved mermaid back?"

Midgard , moved by Nøkken's story, says: "Now I'll show Rán what happens when you make a serpent angry."

Midgard winds closer to the impressive metal gate, which seems like a giant wall between them and the other side. With a confident expression in his eyes and a burst of energy, he takes a deep breath and swings his powerful tail at the gate. Each time he hits, the metal makes a dull sound, and Midgard 's tail vibrates from the impact.

After several attempts, with the gate not moving an inch, Midgard looks breathlessly and puzzled at his tail and then at the immovable gate. He shakes his head and says with a hint of wonder in his voice: "It's almost there; I just need a break."

Skrymir steps forward with a smile and says: "Can't even see a dent in the door." Midgard laughs insincerely. He begins to study the ancient runes engraved on the surface of the gate. After a moment of concentration, he nods to himself. "Strength alone won't get us through; Nøkken's help must be the key."

He takes a deep breath and tightens his grip on his axe. "Will you play one of your beautiful melodies, Nøkken?"

A gentle melody can now be heard in the background. Nøkken, with his long, green locks, sits on a pile of gold with his harp in his lap. His fingers move lightly and elegantly over the strings, as if they were dancing on the water's surface.

The melody, Nøkken's own work, fills the air with enchanting beauty. It's as if each note has the power to enchant anyone who listens. Skrymir, Midgard , and Fenris can't help but stop and be carried away by the music.

As Midgard slowly winds away from the gate, and Nøkken's melody plays in the background, Skrymir steps forward with his axe in hand. With a crooked smile, he looks at the gate and takes a deep breath before giving the gate a controlled blow with his axe.

The gate shakes and almost opens. Skrymir, unfazed by this, looks over at Midgard before swinging the axe again, and the gate opens with a bang. "Sometimes you need more than raw muscle on magic potion," he says with a cheeky tone.
Midgard exclaims, "It was me who broke the gate," "if it wasn't for me having to carry you out of the labyrinth, I would have had enough strength to completely destroy it." The others laugh.

The treasure keeper steps forward from the darkness, his eyes glinting with curiosity and surprise. "I've never seen anyone break through that door before," he says in a deep voice.

Skrymir, Fenris, and Midgard exchange a look. "Would you like to come with us to freedom?" Fenris asks kindly.

"My place is here," he says with a voice that holds wisdom and sadness. "I am the guardian of this treasure, and although freedom is tempting, it is my duty to keep watch."

Skrymir and the others respect his decision and say goodbye with an acknowledging nod. The treasure keeper remains standing, alone in the darkness, his faithful duty unshakable.

They step carefully up the long corridor, where the coldness of the stones penetrates the air. Each step produces a faint echo in the long corridor.

Finally, they reach a heavy door adorned with ancient, engraved symbols. Skrymir takes hold of the handle, and the door creaks reluctantly open. A sudden warmth meets them, and they step into a magnificent throne room, illuminated by faint glimmers from floating light sources on the walls.

At the end of the room sits Ran on her throne, surrounded by the blue-green glow of the underwater depths. Her gaze is cold and calculating, as if she has already assessed their fate.

Ran raises an eyebrow, a smile that is only slightly milder than her previous cold gaze. "It was bound to happen at some point," she says, her voice filled with a mix of surprise and understanding. "To think I trusted that Nøkken could prevent anyone from coming in."

Nøkken looks down at the floor.

Skrymir straightens up and meets her gaze. "Nøkken did play a beautiful melody," he replies, "but as you can see, we were determined to be free."

Fenris nods, "We're not so easily deterred. It takes more than a labyrinth and a locked door to hold us back."

Ran laughs lightly, a sound of respect in her voice. "I can see that. Maybe I should send you by Helheim to see if you can escape that."

Midgard , who has kept to the background, now comes forward with a threatening hiss. "You've wasted my time, and I'll show you what happens when you waste my time." His eyes glint with determination and strength, ready to fight.

Rán laughs again. "I'm glad my husband Ægir isn't home, little serpent ," she says. "For he would probably have stopped me, but now we shall play." Rán rubs her fingers. "Something I have a lot of is gold." "Now you'll see what you can buy with gold."

Rán snaps her fingers, and immediately a large, massive door springs open. Behind it, they can all hear deep, rumbling sounds - the sound of a dragon. Slowly and majestically, the dragon opens the door even more with its huge claws and enters the throne room.

Its shiny scales glimmer in the faint light, and its eyes glow like embers that have been kept lit for centuries.

Skrymir, Fenris, and Midgard stand still, staring at the dragon. Even the always cocky Midgard looks a bit unsure as the dragon takes its place next to Rán.

Rán smiles triumphantly. "I understand from the treasure keeper that you were looking for resistance, little serpent ," she says. "You've come to the right place."

"Nidhogg, show them what a dragon can do," shouts Rán. Nidhogg's roar filled the air like a dark symphony of fear and challenge. His eyes glowed red like the most intense flames, and with each breath, a new wave of fire ignited from his maw.

Skrymir stepped forward, his axe raised high, challenging the dragon with a roar of his own. Nidhogg responded by unleashing a cascade of flames towards Skrymir. With a swift motion of his axe, Skrymir created a barrier of sparks that shielded him from the worst of the heat. He lunged forward and swung at the dragon, but Nidhogg's scales were too strong, and the axe slid off.

Fenris, with his speed and agility, leaped towards the dragon, claws and teeth ready for battle. He tried to bite Nidhogg's wings to weaken his flying ability. The dragon screamed in pain, and with a powerful swipe of its tail, sent Fenris flying through the air, crashing down with a thud.

Midgard , coiling around the dragon, attempted to strangle it. He squeezed tighter and tighter, but Nidhogg was not easily defeated. With a powerful twist, Nidhogg wriggled free from Midgard 's grasp and flung him away with his tail.

The battle continued in an endless stream of attacks and defenses. Skrymir tried again to strike with his axe, this time aiming for Nidhogg's head, but the dragon elegantly dodged. Fenris, still determined, lunged again at the dragon, this time aiming for its neck. Nidhogg screamed and writhed, but Fenris held on until, with a furious jerk, he was thrown off.

Midgard tried a new tactic, coiling around Nidhogg's legs to trip him.

But Nidhogg was wise; he lifted his leg and bit Midgard, causing him to release his grip. With a powerful motion, he flung Midgard away, crashing into a wall with a loud bang. Nidhogg roared triumphantly and sent flames towards Fenris and Skrymir, who had to jump aside to avoid them.

Fenris leaped at the dragon again, but this time Nidhogg snapped at him, catching him with his sharp teeth and tossing him aside like a toy doll. Skrymir tried to attack from another angle, but Nidhogg used his powerful wings to create a wind that blew the giant off balance, causing him to fall.

With a triumphant roar, Nidhogg blasted fire at Midgard, who tried to curl up to protect himself. Midgard's scales turned black and charred, but he was still alive, though weakened and unable to continue fighting.

Skrymir stood up, looking at his friends lying exhausted and wounded. He realized they were outmatched by the dragon and decided on a desperate tactic. Gathering his strength, he hurled his axe with all his might towards Nidhogg's heart. The axe flew through the air, but just before it could strike, Nidhogg changed course, and the axe hit only his scales, causing no damage.

Nidhogg roared triumphantly one last time before, with a powerful flap of his wings, he knocked Skrymir to the ground. Skrymir, Fenris, and Midgard lay scattered in the throne room, exhausted and defeated, but still alive.

Rán, majestically seated on her throne, looked down at the three beaten Vættir. Her eyes, deep as the darkest oceans, pierced them with a mix of triumph and disdain. With a voice that rolled like the waves on the ocean's surface, she declared:

"Sparing your lives is the exception, not the rule." Let this be a warning to all who would consider opposing the queen of the sea. Tell the world of this day, of the battle you lost, and the humiliation you suffered. May your story serve as a reminder of my power and the price paid for crossing me."

Midgard, Fenris, and Skrymir, still exhausted from the battle, nodded weakly, understanding the gravity of Rán's words. Rán let a smile play across her lips and made a cold, calculating gesture. "Go now," she said, "and let the world hear of the queen of the sea."

Rán then turned to Nøkken, "And you, Nøkken, I can no longer trust you," she motioned to one of the guards: "Chain him to my throne; he shall be entertainment."

Nøkken looked lost, first towards the three defeated, then towards the mermaid. His lost expression turned to a smile, and a glimmer of hope appeared in his eyes. He had now emerged from the treasury, close to his beloved. He looked back at the three and gave them a grateful nod.

The three survivors, though defeated, turned and left the throne room. They moved through the long corridors, back to the entrance they had come through, and out through the portal to the sea again, floating up, pulled by a mix of disappointment and relief.

As they surfaced, Fenris and Skrymir jumped onto Midgard's back. They didn't speak. Skrymir could hear Midgard muttering to himself, "Should have drunk more of that magic potion," "I'll show that dragon when I get back," "If only I had wings like that, I would have won."

Skrymir mustered his courage and said to Midgard, "We can't win every time; we should just be glad we survived." "Shut up," Midgard replied. "Once I've dropped you off, I'll find a wizard to turn me into a dragon, and then Nidhogg will see. I'll throw him all the way to Helheim. It's unfair that he has wings, claws, and fire."

On Midgard's back, the three friends continued their journey through the deep waters. After a while, they began to glimpse something large and impressive on the horizon. The closer they got, the clearer it became: A massive ship, constructed not of wood and sailcloth as we know it, but of solid stone.

The ship rested majestically in the water like a giant rock in the sea. Its hull was carved from dark granite, polished to a shining gleam by the passage of time. Complex patterns and symbols engraved all over the ship's surface told a story older than time itself. These runes and figures, created with depth and precision that spoke of masterful craftsmanship, glowed faintly in the gentle light from the ocean's surface.

The ship's bow was shaped like a sea monster, with an open mouth and sharp, engraved teeth stretching towards the sky as a challenge to the world. The mast, tall and proud, stood in the middle of the deck, made of a massive stone pillar twined with twisted strands of seaweed and sea grass, winding up towards the sky as a living part of the ship.

The few windows on the ship were not made of glass but of transparent stone, allowing the deep blue sea light to stream in and cast plays of light inside the ship. Impressive statues of sea Vættir stood all over the deck, each detail meticulously carved from the same dark granite that made up the ship's hull.

The stone ship was not just a vessel but a work of art, a tribute to the power and mystery of the sea, standing as a monument to the eternal movement and beauty of time.

As the three friends admired the impressive stone ship floating calmly in the water, a hatch on the side of the ship opened. A giant figure emerged, tall and strong, dressed in furrowed clothes made of bearskin.

"Ahoy!" the giant called out with a voice that rolled like thunder over the water. "Who do we have here? Three adventurous souls on the sea's expanse?"

Fenris, Skrymir, and Midgard looked up in surprise at the giant, who grinned mischievously down at them.

"You look like you're in need of adventure," the giant continued, "and I have an adventure that will set your hearts aflame with excitement! Who wants to join the hunt for the golden walrus from Norse mythology?" "It's said to hold a treasure unlike any seen before!"

Fenris' eyes sparkled with interest, while Skrymir looked skeptically at the giant. Midgard shifted impatiently in the water.

"That sounds exciting," said Skrymir with a wink, "I should really visit a friend, but there's always time for a little adventure!"

Midgard let out a deep, disappointed sound, while the other two looked at each other in surprise. After a moment of silence, Midgard said, "No more adventures until I have wings and can spit fire!" and began to swim away from the ship.

The giant looked puzzled and waved goodbye with his giant hand as the three friends continued their journey along the great river.

Chapter 9: The Realm of Thorgar

The three travelers continued swimming on Midgard's back, navigating through the deep and mysterious waters of the great river. After hours on the water, the outlines of a wide bay began to take shape ahead. The water shifted from deep blue to a subdued turquoise, with sunlight reflecting off the waves in small glimmers.

The bay was surrounded by high, rocky shores where lush forests dressed the landscape up the mountainsides. At the end of the bay, they could see the silhouette of towers and walls marking the beginning of Thorgar's realm. The towers stood like guards, overseeing the entrance to the mysterious land, and the walls were built of massive stones that testified to a kingdom of great strength and beauty.

Midgard stopped at the entrance to the bay and turned towards the three travelers. "Here we are," it said with a deep rumble from the depths. "Thorgar's realm lies just ahead. Take care of yourselves inside; now that I am not there to protect you." "And next time we meet, I will have wings!" The other two laughed, thanked for the help, and jumped down from the back. The great serpent dove deep into the water and disappeared as the waves slowly settled.

The two friends turned their attention to the inviting bay in front of them. With determined steps, they walked into the shallower water and moved toward the land. The water was clear and shone in the sunlight, and beneath them, they could see colorful fish swimming past in a ballet of movements.

As they reached the shore, they felt the firmness of the earth under their feet again. The surrounding forest was dense and full of life, with trees so tall they reached up towards the sky like proud guards. The sound of birdsong filled the air, and insects buzzed around them in a constant humming melody.

They began to move up the stony path that led them to Thorgard's castle. With each step, their anticipation of what awaited them grew.

The sun shone through the foliage, and small patches of light danced on the ground as if nature itself celebrated their arrival.

Skrymir, with his large axe over his shoulder, led the way. His steps were firm and determined as he carefully navigated through the forest's labyrinth. Fenris, with his pointed snout and sharp eyes, was on alert, attentive to any sound or movement around them.

As they moved forward, the forest atmosphere grew denser and more mysterious. They heard the rustling of the wind through the treetops and the sounds of animals hidden in the dense foliage. Occasionally, they sensed hidden Vættir watching them from the shadows, but they remained invisible and undefined.

After several hours of hiking, they finally came to a clearing in the forest. Before them rose an impressive stone gate, with engraved runes and patterns that shone in the gentle light. Above the gate was Thorgard's emblem, a mighty eagle surrounded by lightning bolts.

Skrymir stopped and examined the gate. He drew his axe and studied the runes closely. "This is where we enter," he said in a deep voice.

Fenris nodded, and together they approached the gate. With a burst of spiritual energy, the gate slowly opened for them, as if the forest itself welcomed them into Thorgard's realm.

They continued and approached a clearing where they thought they had arrived, but the atmosphere changed immediately. The golden rays of the sun penetrated the forest, and it was here that the first signs of disturbance began to show.

In the middle of the clearing, a scene of a battleground unfolded before them. Fallen trees lay scattered, their trunks broken in uneven pieces and their branches split as after a violent collision.

Some of the oldest and largest trees in the forest, which once stood like giant watchtowers over the forest floor, now burned and charred. Charred stripes ran down their trunks, and parts of their branches and tops were reduced to ash. It looked as if lightning itself had struck them, but to an extent and intensity rarely seen.

The forest floor was also dotted with signs of battle: Veils of fabric hanging from trees as remnants of a hasty retreat, and weapons, some broken, others lost in haste.

In some places, the ground was torn up as after a powerful explosion, and small stones and clumps of earth lay scattered around. It was clear that there had been an intense and violent confrontation, and they could only imagine what had taken place here before their arrival.

The battleground stretched as far as the eye could see. Fallen trees, broken branches, and signs of battle were visible everywhere. There was an almost indescribable intensity in the air, as if the past battle still lingered in the air as an unspoken warning.

At the end of the large battleground, a mountain rose majestically. It was a mountain of pure granite that glistened and shone in the sun's rays. The sharp contrast between the dark, raw fallen trees in the clearing and the shining mountain created a breathtaking sight. The mountainside was rough and uneven with deep cracks and crevices, as if time itself had left its marks on it.

The shadows on the peak shifted like waves on the sea, and its contours were sharply outlined against the blue sky. It was as if the mountainside itself was a story, a silent witness to the passage of time and the events that had taken place here through the millennia.

In the middle of the mountainside, embedded as part of the massive granite landscape, one could sense a cave that was carved into the mountain itself. The structure of the cave was impressive; its large entrance seemed almost to meld with the mountain's natural forms, as if it had grown out of the stone itself.

The walls of the cave were solidly built of granite blocks that matched the mountain's natural shades. Among the robust structure of the walls were inserted windows with leaded glass that reflected the sunlight and added a glint of color to the otherwise gray facade. The gates to the cave were heavy and massive, and there was a feeling of impregnability about them.

The sound of a guard's horn could be heard in the distance, and although it was a remote cave, one could sense its significance and power. The presence of the cave was both a tribute to the giants' ability to shape and adapt to nature and a reminder of the giants' pride and determination.

They moved cautiously through the rugged landscape, where burnt and fallen trees lay scattered as mute witnesses of previous battles. Each step was surrounded by a strange, pressing rustle, as if the tumult of the past still hung in the air. They looked up towards the mountainside, where the mighty cave cut into the granite's shining surface.

The path up to the cave's entrance was covered with stones and gravel, as if nature itself had tried to hide the entrance. They approached the cave's entrance and could begin to see the contours on the facade. It was not just a rough and uneven surface; the stone was beautifully carved with intricate patterns and symbols. Each notch and curl in the stone was created with care and skill, as if it told a story from a distant past.

The sculptural details depicted figures from Norse mythology: giants, animals, and mystical symbols. The deep carvings cast shadows that gave the cave's entrance an almost living expression, as if the ancient stone itself had something to tell.

Above the entrance to the cave hung a thick, green moss curtain that moved lightly in the cooling wind. The green moss stood out as a contrast to the gray stone, and it seemed as if the moss had found a way to live in symbiosis with the stone-cold surface.

Skrymir and Fenris could not help but admire the craftsmanship behind this entrance. It was like standing in front of a work of art, where every detail was thought out with care and love for the craft.

From the depths of the cave, one could hear a distant rumble and a faint echo of sounds that indicated life behind the massive facade. It sounded as if there was activity inside the cave, as if it hid secrets and mysteries waiting to be discovered. The sound of voices mumbling and footsteps scraping against the stone floor could be sensed behind the thick walls, adding to the mystique surrounding this place.

With some caution, they approached the beautifully carved cave entrance. Skrymir reached out and knocked gently on the massive stone door. After a moment of waiting, they heard a voice behind the door.

A hatch in the door was cautiously pushed open, and a pair of sharp eyes peeked curiously out. Behind the hatch opening stood an older giant with gray beard and deep wrinkles in his face. His hair was wild and tangled, as if it had not seen a comb in years. With a skeptical look, he asked, "Who are you, and what do you want here?"

Skrymir stepped forward and briefly introduced them: "I am Skrymir, and this is Fenris. We are here to meet Thorgar."

The older giant looked them over for a moment, as if considering whether they were worthy to enter their secret realm. Finally, he nodded slowly and said, "Come inside. Thorgar has spoken of your arrival. I will show you the way."

With a creak, the hatch opening was closed, and the door began to slide slowly aside, revealing a dark corridor into the depths of the cave.

They stepped into the cave's dim interior, where the air was cold and damp, and the light from the clear day outside was quickly replaced by a subdued glow from torches burning along the walls. The corridor was wide and high, and the stones around them were rough and unpolished, as if they had been hewn with powerful blows from an ancient tool.

The sound of their steps echoed in the heavy stones, and a faint echo made it sound as if there was more life than just themselves in this ancient cave. The walls were covered with natural formations, as if time itself had created patterns in the stone – it was like walking through nature's own art gallery.

The older giant led them with sure steps through the labyrinth of corridors, and although the path was uneven and often twisted in unexpected directions, it seemed as if he knew every nook and cranny of this underground world.

As they moved deeper into the cave, the sound of their steps was muffled by the soft, dry earth beneath them. But as they continued, a distant hum began to reach their ears – a mix of laughter, singing, and musical tones that grew in strength with each step they took closer.

The coldness of the corridor and the dim lighting were replaced by a warmer and more inviting light that came from a nearby opening. The lively atmosphere and the warm glow from the torches created an almost magical mood in the hall, and it was clear that they had come to a place where festivity and joy were an important part of everyday life.

The feast was in full swing, and the hall buzzed with life and energy. Colorful banners hung down from the ceiling, and their colors were tossed around the room by flickering torches. The large wooden tables, covered with lavish platters of food and drink, served as gathering points for the partygoers.

The music filled the air with a lively melody, played on old, carved instruments by musicians in the corner of the hall. Their tunes made people stomp in time, clink their mugs, and sing along to the old songs. Some danced in the middle of the hall in a fast, wild dance, while others sat in groups and shared stories and laughter over food and drink.

The smells from the food filled the air – spicy meat dishes, fresh vegetables, and baked goods with sweet spices. Drinking horns were filled and refilled with a golden liquid that made laughter flow even more freely.

Everywhere in the hall, one could feel a sense of camaraderie and festive spirit, as if everyone, regardless of background or origin, was gathered in the spirit of community to celebrate.

The giants in Thorgard's hall were an impressive and somewhat intimidating sight. They were large, almost twice as tall as humans, and their muscular bodies were covered with worn battle uniforms. Most wore armor made of animal skins and heavy leather trousers, but many also had bloodstains and tears in their equipment, clearly showing that they had recently been in battle.

The heavy metal helmets, some with horns or animal skulls as decorations, sat askew on their heads. Their hands were rough and full of scrapes, and they bore signs of recent wounds and bruises. Their faces were worn, with scars, sweaty foreheads, and large teeth.

Even though the giants looked tired and worn after battle, they still radiated a kind of calm and dignity. They moved with a confidence that came from knowing who they were and what they were worth. Behind their rugged exteriors, one could sense a spark of warmth and pride, as if each giant carried a story that was waiting to be told.

Thorgard almost leaped down from his throne with an energy and speed that surprised everyone in the hall. His large steps sounded heavy on the stone floor, and his armor clinked lightly as he ran. His face lit up in a big smile, and his eyes sparkled with joy and recognition as he approached.

His hair, long and wild, flew behind him as he ran. Thorgard was dressed in an armor of golden metal that reflected the light from the torches and gave him an almost divine glow.

As he reached them, he stopped abruptly and took a deep breath to recover. His hands rested on his knees as he breathed heavily. "Skrymir! Fenris! It's good to see you," he exclaimed with a deep and resonant voice that filled the entire room.

Thorgard straightened up and with a broad smile, he extended a large hand towards his wife Grid, who approached with two large drinking horns.

"Come, let us drink to the reunion and the adventures that await us!" said Thorgard with a warmth in his voice that made the room buzz with anticipation.

The drinking horns were adorned with intricate patterns and engravings that told of old battles and victories. The contents of the horns glinted in the flickering light from the torches and smelled of honey and spices.

He lifted his own horn and held it out to Skrymir and Fenris. "To the honor of friendship and adventure!" he said with a smile before taking a deep sip of the drink.

Thorgard led them to a long, sturdy wooden table that stood in the middle of the room. They sat down, and Thorgard filled their mugs with a frothy drink from a large wooden jug in the middle of the table.

"Tell me about your experiences," said Thorgard curiously, as he took a sip of his drink. "I am very interested in hearing about your adventures."

Skrymir began to tell about their journey on the river, about Nøkken and the epic battle against the mysterious dragon Nidhogg. His story was filled with details about the intensity of the battle, and how they discovered the treasure chamber.

Fenris added by describing the treasure chamber with its lavish wealth and the huge axe they found there. He told about how they were tested by Ran and about their journey on Midgard through the labyrinthine dungeon.

Thorgard listened intently as they told their story, nodding occasionally and occasionally exclaiming "impressive!" or "that must have been an experience!" When they were finished, he said, "Your adventure sounds both dangerous and exciting. You have truly proven your worth."

With a smile on his lips, Thorgard added, "There is a new adventure waiting for you outside. An adventure that makes Nidhogg seem like a fly."

Thorgard put his mug down and looked seriously at Skrymir and Fenris. "There is something you should know," he began. "We are in battle with Thor himself."

Skrymir and Fenris exchanged a surprised look. "The god of thunder?" "The mighty Aesir god known for his unparalleled strength and unshakable will?" Exclaimed Skrymir

"Yes," continued Thorgard, "that is the reason for the destruction outside. Thor has sent thunder and lightning down on our land, and we must defend ourselves."

Fenris scratched his beard and said, "That doesn't sound like the Thor we know from the old sagas. Why would he attack?"

Thorgard sighed deeply. "I really don't know". "He keeps shouting that I have the potion of eternal death. But I haven't taken any potion from him. Don't know what he's talking about."

Skrymir looked questioning. "Wonder what he means." "How can we help?"

Thorgard smiled crookedly and said "Tomorrow when the sun rises, you must join us on the battlefield." "He may not get any potion, but he can get a fight"

Thorgard smiled broadly and reached for a large jug filled with golden mead, which he then handed to Skrymir. "Drink, and let's celebrate like old friends," he said.

Fenris received a large bowl filled with a darker, more robust drink that smelled of the deep secrets of the forest. He lifted the bowl in a gesture of respect and drank deeply.

Finally, Thorgard took his large mug and raised it towards the ceiling. "May we send Thor back where he came from!" he shouted out in the hall.

With that, they toasted, and the music began to play. The giants in the hall clapped in time, and soon everyone was in a festive mood. Skrymir and Fenris quickly got caught up in the lively atmosphere and celebrated with Thorgard and his people.

The next morning, Skrymir woke up with a heavy headache and a slight buzzing in his head. His eyes were a bit more narrow, and his voice had a deeper tone than usual. He stretched and rubbed his temples. "Ah, the work of mead," he muttered with a crooked smile.

Other giants in the castle could also feel the effects of the previous night's festivities. Some complained of thirst, while others tried to find a cure for their headaches. Fenris, perhaps not as used to giant mead, was still resting, with half-open eyes and a slightly grumpy expression.

Thorgard, with his robust nature, seemed to fare a bit better than the others. He sat up and stretched before noticing Skrymir's condition with a smile. "Ah, the joys of a party," he said with a wink.

As the morning sun began to shine through the air ducts in Thorgard's hall, the giants gathered around the large long table in the middle of the room. The table was made of solid wood and stretched almost from one end of the hall to the other.

The giants wore their battle uniforms, worn and marked by the trials of battle. Iron and leather armors, helmets with horns, and shields bearing scars from previous battles were all signs of their warrior lifestyle.

In a distant corner, Grid stood by her giant pots, steaming and sizzling over a blazing fire. She stirred energetically in the bubbling dishes with her large iron glove, which roared and sputtered in the glowing light.

Grid was known for her cooking among the giants. Her creations were always filled with flavor and nutrition, and her love for details was evident in every dish. She worked with a devotion and precision that could only be matched by her own strength.

As she worked, she sang softly to herself, her voice filled with a mix of power and grace. Her long hair fell in dark curls down her shoulders, and her eyes sparkled with deep wisdom and calm.

In the pots, Grid mixed ingredients from all over the giant world: juicy meat pieces from the wildest animals, knobby roots and vegetables

Chapter 10: The Mighty Thor

They all stood in a line outside the cave. Skrymir stood right behind Thorgard, with Fenris by his side. The morning was cool, and dew lay like a thin layer over the grass and surrounding trees. The sun slowly began to rise over the horizon, casting its soft, golden light over the landscape. In front of the cave, where the warriors gathered, there was a tense atmosphere.

The stones and rocks around the cave lit up in the morning sun's glow, and a light morning fog hung over the ground, adding a mysterious and challenging feel to the place. There was a silence only broken by the song of birds and the sound of the wind blowing through the trees.

The warriors stood together, their faces serious but resolutely determined. They had mentally prepared for today's battle against Thor, the mighty god with his hammer, Mjolnir. Although they were nervous, there was also a sense of community and strength among them.

Skrymir slowly lifted his gaze and fixed it on Thor, and instantly all the hangovers from yesterday's feast disappeared. At the end of the battlefield, Thor sat majestically on his goat, Tanngnjóstr. Thor was an imposing figure in the distant light from the sun, which shone behind him and cast a halo around him.

Thor's powerful body was covered in a tunic dyed deep red, symbolizing his fierce nature and warrior spirit. His muscles were well-defined and bulging, reflecting the incredible strength he possessed.

His long, flowing hair, golden as the sun itself, fell over his broad shoulders in a wild mane. His eyes, deep and intense as the depths of the sea, shone with an inner fire of determination and power. His beard was thick and unruly, giving him a wild and invincible appearance.

Thor sat upright and unyielding, with a firm grip on his hammer, ready to face the giants. His presence alone radiated authority and superiority, and although Skrymir was a strong and fearless giant himself, he couldn't help but feel a certain awe towards the mighty Thor.

Skrymir focused on the hammer, Mjolnir, which Thor held in his hand. The hammer was unlike any other hammer Skrymir had ever seen before. It was compact and sturdy, made of the finest iron and engraved with ancient runes that pulsed with magic.

Mjolnir's shape was simple yet powerful, with a short, thick shaft and a large, square hammerhead. Despite its apparent weight, the hammer seemed almost effortlessly carried by Thor, as if it were an extension of himself.

It was surrounded by a sparkling aura, and its surface glimmered in the morning sun with an almost electric sheen. Skrymir could feel the intense energy emanating from the hammer, and even though he was a mighty giant, he couldn't help but feel a deep reverence for this powerful artifact.

Mjolnir was not just a weapon; it was a symbol of Thor's incomparable strength, his unshakeable will, and his fearless courage. It was clear to Skrymir that he was not just fighting a man, but a god whose power was unlike anything else in the nine worlds.

Thor straightened up in his saddle, Mjolnir resting in his hand with its powerful presence. His eyes, glowing with determination, scanned the assembled giants with an intensity that made the air vibrate.

With a deep, resounding voice that carried through the morning fog's silence, Thor shouted to the giants, "Giants, feel my power and understand my resolve! Give me the eternal death potion now if you wish to avoid the battle that awaits you. I have not come here to kill without reason, but to find a fair solution."

His words were like thunderclaps that cut through the air, and his tone was both challenging and serious. He stood there, a mighty god, surrounded by the aura of Mjolnir, and his presence alone was a reminder of his unmatched strength and power.

Although Thor offered a chance for settlement, there was no doubt that he was ready to fight if the giants did not meet his demands. His shout was a clear demonstration of his authority and his willingness to protect the gods by any means necessary.

Thorgard stepped forward from the ranks of giants and stood up to his full height.

"Thor," Thorgard shouted back, his eyes meeting Thor's intense gaze, "I don't know what you mean by the eternal death potion. We don't have such a drink with us, and I have never heard of anything like that."

His voice carried sincere confusion, and his hands were open and visible as signs of his innocence. "We are here to defend our honor and our land. If you seek another solution than battle, then let us find a way forward together. But the eternal death potion, we do not have it."

"There is nothing else to do but to take the potion by force," he said as he dismounted his goat Tanngnjóstr. There was silence as if all of Jotunheim held its breath and waited for what would happen next.

On one side of the battlefield stood Thorgard with Skrymir and Fenris by his side. They were ready for battle, their battle uniforms tight around their muscles, and their eyes sharp as the edge of a knife. Skrymir's large axe rested heavily over his shoulder, while Fenris' claws shone in the subdued light from the sky. Behind them stood the giants, their massively built figures filling the sky with their menacing presence.

In front of them, on the opposite side of the open space, stood Thor with Mjolnir raised, ready to throw. The clouds gathered around him, and suddenly, there was a bang as if the whole mountain exploded. The bang was followed by a bolt of lightning, followed by a scream, and a giant flying back. Mjolnir had been thrown and hit right in the chest of one of the great giants.

"Attack!" shouted Thorgard. As he ran towards Thor and all the giants followed.

On the open battlefield, the giants began to run towards Thor, resembling a wave of evil. With a roar of war joy, they steered directly towards Thor, each one convinced that their strength and courage would bring them victory over the god and secure the barrel of mead.

But in their eagerness to be the one to fell Thor, they came closer and closer to each other until they were so tightly packed that they could no longer move freely. Skrymir, Fenris, and the other giants stumbled over each other in a chaotic mass of combat and confusion.

Thor saw the opportunity and seized it immediately. With Mjolnir raised high above his head, he threw his hammer directly into the crowd of giants. Lightning leaped from the hammer, and with a bang, it hit several of them, causing them to fall to the ground.

In the midst of all this chaos stood Thorgard, shaking with rage and disappointment over the giants' uncoordinated attack. He shouted and tried to gather his troops, but it was too late. Thor took advantage of the giants' mistake and directed his attack against them. It was a quick and devastating battle. Although the giants were strong and numerous, they were divided, and Thor had an advantage in the open landscape.

"Into the forest," shouted Thorgard, and the giants who could still fight ran into the forest.

"Do you think the forest can save you?" shouted Thor and threw Mjolnir, leveling all the trees in its path.

Skrymir ran behind a tree, where he could catch his breath. Meanwhile, he could hear giants running wildly towards Thor, upon which they were flung through the air by Mjolnir shortly after. How will we ever get a hit on Thor, Skrymir thought to himself. He turned and looked behind the tree.

Thor stepped into the forest, where the dense crowns of the trees cast long shadows on the ground. The forest was quiet, but a sense of anticipation hung in the air like a thick fog. Between the tree trunks, he could glimpse figures moving in hiding, their eyes glinting in the dark, like wild animals ready to attack.

With a roar, the giants burst forth from their hiding places, their battle cries echoing between the trees. They stormed towards Thor with shouts and roars, their weapons raised and ready for battle. But for each giant who tried to attack him, Thor swung his mighty hammer, Mjolnir, and struck them with unimaginable power.

The giants were thrown back like leaves in the wind, some fell to the ground with a bang, others were sent back against the trees, where they hit with a loud sound. Despite their numbers and their courage, they could not withstand Mjolnir's unmatched power.

Thor stood unshakable in the midst of the forest's chaos, his breath heavy, and sweat beading on his forehead, but his gaze was firm, and his hammer still swung. The remaining giants retreated, defeated and scared, while Thor stood victorious, the ruler of the forest and its challenges.

Skrymir clenched the shaft of his axe, and sweat began to bead down from his forehead. Thoughts swirled.
"Is it time to run towards Thor?"
"I have to try to attack him, otherwise, I can't show my face in the cave again."
"Where is Fenris?"
"I can hear he's getting closer, if I sneak around the tree when he walks by, I can get behind him"
Skrymir sneaked behind the tree while Thor walked by.
"Good, it worked," thought Skrymir. He looked at Thor's back, thinking about when it was best to run towards him.
"He's just a monster," "as if you can sense how much power there is in the god"

Suddenly there was a bang "there he threw Mjolnir, this is my chance" Skrymir took off and ran towards Thor.

In an unexpected turn in the battle, while Thor concentrated on the giants he faced, he suddenly heard a rattling sound behind him. Before he could react, Skrymir came running from behind at high speed, his giant body casting a shadow over Thor, who was fully occupied watching if his hammer hit the advancing giants.

Skrymir's attack was quick and unexpected. With a roar, he swung his giant axe towards Thor, who had just thrown Mjolnir, and was therefore defenseless.

Thor turned around and parried the swing from the axe with his hands. There was a bang through the forest when Skrymir's axe and Thor's gloves Járngreipr met. Thor caught the blow with his bare hands but was pushed backward by Skrymir's strength, and the dust from the forest floor whirled around them.

He struggled to find his footing as he tried to recover from the surprise attack. With an angry shout, Thor gathered himself and stood facing Skrymir with a clenched fist, ready to continue the fight.

Skrymir raised the axe and prepared for another blow, which Thor again parried with his gloves. Thor began to laugh, "It's been a long time since someone got a hit on me," "well done unknown giant, but now it's my turn"

At that moment, there was a bang, and Mjolnir was in Thor's hand. Thorgard swung his axe again, but Thor knocked it out of his hand, where the shaft broke, leaving Skrymir standing with a stump in his hand.

The last thing Skrymir saw was Thor preparing for a swing, and then he could hear a loud bang. It sounded like lightning struck. Everything went black for his eyes, and he was flung through the air.

He now lay at the foot of a tree. All the air had disappeared from his body, and he gasped for breath. It was as if his lungs had collapsed, but little by little, he came to himself. He looked up, and there stood mighty Thor, laughing.

"Thanks for the fight, Giant, but no one can match Mjolnir," he said, looking at the hammer. Suddenly he turned red in the face with rage. "You have damaged my gloves!" "How can such an insignificant giant damage gloves made of magical iron?"

"Do you know what I have to go through to get those wretched dwarves to repair these gloves," "you won't escape alive from this." "Thor walked angrily towards Skrymir, with fire in his eyes and his hand clenched around Mjolnir."

Skrymir looked around for something to defend himself with, but

there was nothing. He tried to get up, but he hadn't caught his breath yet.
"What do I do?" thought Skrymir. "I can't die now! I haven't even tried to kiss a giant girl."

Suddenly Fenris came running with Thorgard on his back, and Thorgard delivered a blow to Thor, which he parried with Mjolnir. "There you are, give me the death potion," shouted Thor and walked towards the thicket, which Thorgard ran into with Fenris.

A group of giants ran towards Thor, which he sent in each direction. Thorgard and Fenris came jumping through a bush and delivered another blow to Thor, which he barely managed to parry, after which he threw Mjolnir at them. Mjolnir whizzed through the air and hit just next to.
The hammer stopped in the air and flew back towards Thor. He stretched out his arm to catch the hammer, but it flew out of the glove.
"Cursed gloves," whispered Thor to himself, and looked after Mjolnir.
Here, Thorgard saw his chance to reorganize. "To the cave," shouted Thorgard, and all the giants who could still get up ran towards the cave.

"Where are you going?" shouted Thor. He began to walk briskly towards Mjolnir. He went over and picked up Mjolnir. While he grumbled, "Must get hold of those dwarves."

Skrymir tried to get up, but he still couldn't breathe properly, and his legs were like rubber.

He looked at Thor, who swung his hammer and flew towards the giants.

"I hope they reached the cave," thought Skrymir. He tried to lift himself, but nothing helped. "I must help them," but how? I can't breathe.

Out of the bush came Fenris, with a smile. "Fenriiiis," exclaimed Skrymir. Fenris ran happily over to Skrymir, wagging his tail a bit.

"Did they get to safety?" asked Skrymir,

"Yes, they all made it into the cave. Thorgard told me it was part of the plan" The cave is enchanted, so they have plans to tire Thor out there."

Fenris, with his sharp senses, listened carefully and stared in the direction of the cave with a look full of anticipation and a hint of fear. Fenris, pricked his ears and growled softly. "Thor, is by the cave."

The blows on the door became faster and more violent, as if Thor's anger could not be contained. "Do you think it will hold, we must help them," said Skrymir, his voice trembling with both excitement and fear.

"Thorgard said that nothing could open that gate" so you don't have to be afraid. You just have to come to yourself, then everything will be fine.

The blows on the door intensified, dark clouds gathered, and you could hear lightning and thunder. Every time Thor hit the door, there was a bang so loud that you would think he was throwing a moon at the mountain. The bangs were followed by sound waves that whizzed between the trees.

Skrymir looked nervously at Fenris. Suddenly there was a big flash of light that lit up the forest, followed by a big gust of wind, and then a howling tone.

The forest fell completely silent. It ran cold down Skrymir's back. "He has opened the gate," he exclaimed.

Yes, answered Fenris. We must help them, can you get up?

Skrymir tried to get up, but his legs gave way under him. I need to take some of the magic potion, he said, and took out the bottle. He unscrewed the lid.

"Would you like some?" he asked, handing the bottle to Fenris. "No thanks" I've had such dark dreams since I got a sip from the old lady.

"That sounds strange," remarked Skrymir. "But we must save the giants." He took a sip from the bottle, felt the energy flow through his body, and grew a little in height. After getting up, he stretched and walked over to the remains of his hammer. As he picked up the axe head with the wooden stump, he said. "let's save our friends"

As he said those words, they could hear another bang, but the bang sounded like it came outside the cave.
Skrymir looked with scared eyes at Fenris, "he can't already have defeated everyone in the cave?"
Another bang sounded, and dust and forest floor flew up. Fenris and Skrymir now looked at Thor, who stood bent forward, with his left knuckle in the forest floor. "Damn gloves," he exclaimed in an irritated tone.

Thor lifted his hammer and pointed it towards Skrymir, "you there, Giant!" "You will pay for having damaged my gloves!"
Fenris thought quickly, grabbed Skrymir, and threw him on his back.

Thor began to swing his hammer and prepared to throw it at Skrymir and Fenris. He threw the hammer, but Fenris just managed to jump over it, and it continued through a tree.
"Must be the gloves, I never miss normally," muttered Thor to himself. Thor made a whistle, and Tanngnjóstr was quickly on his way.

In the dark and dense forest in Jötunheimen, which had stood still for many hundreds of years, you could now hear the sound of fast hooves and crunching leaves. Thor, the mighty god with his hammer Mjolnir in hand, in wild pursuit of Tanngnjóstr, his faithful companion.
Further ahead of them in the forest, Fenris ran with his fast and cunning movement, trying to escape Thor and Tanngnjóstr's relentless pursuit. The sound of crunching branches and rustling leaves filled the air as they continued their wild chase.

Skrymir looked back and could see Thor with a big smile and murder in his eyes. Tanngnjóstr had a cold and focused focus, as if he had set Fenris in focus and would never let him out of sight.

Skrymir shouted to Fenris, "We must find a way out of this forest, otherwise Thor will catch up with us!"

Fenris nodded and changed direction, leading them deeper into the forest in an attempt to confuse their pursuers.
But Thor was not so easily fooled. With Mjolnir in hand, he continued to follow them, guided by Tanngnjóstr's sure instincts and his tireless will to catch the escaped giants.

Fenris could begin to hear hooves galloping behind him. "I'd like some of the magic potion now," shouted Fenris. Skrymir handed the bottle down to Fenris's mouth, who took a sip.
Skrymir felt a jerk in Fenris, and the speed was increased.

After several hours of intense pursuit, the forest began to get denser,

Chapter 11: Bergelmir

Thor raised Mjolnir high into the air, gazing skyward. Dark clouds gathered around his lifted arm, thundering and roaring. Lightning began to strike Mjolnir, accompanied by loud thunderclaps.

Suddenly, a massive explosion sounded, and the earth shook violently. The ground beneath Thor disappeared, and he fell through the crack, landing deep in a trench.

The entire mountain trembled, and rocks flew about. Skrymir looked up towards the peak and could make out a face forming. Another explosion echoed, and Thor shot up from the crack, landing some distance from Skrymir.

A distinct face now appeared on the mountainside, and a rumbling sound followed. "Who dares disturb my eternal slumber?" boomed a dark, rumbling voice from the mountain.

Thor stopped and looked up at the awakened mountain with awe in his eyes. Even the mighty god was impressed by the fierce power of nature, now stirred to life in the mountain.

From deep within the mountain, a deep, resonant voice sounded, like tones from nature's own symphony. "Who dares to wake me from my sleep?" the mountain asked with a voice so deep it shook the ground beneath Thor's feet.

Thor, always ready for a confrontation, responded firmly, "It is I, Thor, son of Odin. I pursue this insignificant giant and his wolf."

The mountain paused as if considering Thor's words. "Be careful, Thor, son of Odin," the mountain finally spoke. "Even the mightiest can find themselves ensnared by nature's fury."

With those words, the ground under Thor's feet rolled one last time before calming.

Standing before the imposing mountain, Thor could feel a deep anger emanating from the ancient mountain. The stone face expressed a kind of rage and sorrow he had seldom seen in a mountain before.

"You woke me from a deep sleep, Thor, and for what?" the stone face rumbled, its voice filling the valley. "To remind me of the terrible fate my giant brethren suffered at the hands of the gods?"

Thor bowed his head in respect, realizing he was facing a powerful and ancient being. "I understand your grief, Bergelmir," he replied, "but we had no other choice. Ymir was a threat to both gods and men."

Bergelmir's stone face darkened, and his growl filled the valley like thunder. "My old friend Ymir," he said with a voice filled with pain. "He was part of this world, just as I am. And you gods chose to remove him as if he were merely an obstacle in your path."

Thor could feel Bergelmir's sorrow and anger and felt deep sympathy for the ancient mountain. "I understand your grief, Bergelmir," Thor repeated, "and I am not here to bring more destruction. I seek only to punish the giant who has caused me suffering."

Bergelmir's growling subsided slightly, but his anger was still evident. "Be careful, Thor," he warned. "For my roots stretch deep into the earth, and I will not hesitate to use my power to protect my giant brethren from any threat, even one like you."

With those words, Bergelmir's anger lessened somewhat, but Thor knew he had awakened a potentially dangerous enemy.

Thor stood firm on the ground, facing Bergelmir's now fully visible face and intense gaze. With his golden hair and mighty Mjolnir in hand, he stood tall and said firmly, "Beware, Bergelmir. I am not here to fight you, but if you choose to stand in my way, I will not hesitate to defend myself."

Bergelmir's deep, shaking laughter filled the valley like an earthquake. "Do you really think you can threaten me, little god?" he roared, raising his enormous stone arm to attack.

With a clash of stone against stone, Bergelmir raised his massive arm and swung it towards Thor. Thor quickly parried with Mjolnir, and a sharp flash of light filled the air as the two forces met in a shower of sparks and stone shards.

As the blows fell and shook the surrounding forest, Thor's goats, Tanngnjóstr and Tanngrisnir, emerged from the shadows. With their impressive strength and speed, they tried to distract Bergelmir while Thor gathered his thoughts and prepared for his next move.

However, Bergelmir was not easily distracted. With each strike he sent towards Thor, the earth and trees rolled under his wrath. But Thor was an experienced warrior and a master at defense. He dodged and blocked each of Bergelmir's attacks with skill and strength.

Bergelmir rose up, his form like a living rock wall. His eyes glinted with a deep, inner rage that matched the earthquake's force. He reminded Thor of the gods' killing of his friend Ymir, and now he was ready for revenge.

Thor stood firm, his hammer Mjolnir tightly gripped in his hand. He swung his hammer towards Bergelmir with a powerful motion. But Bergelmir was quick and parried the blow with his own strength, creating a shockwave that sent tremors through the forest.

The two giants fought with an intensity that created storms in the forest. Every movement, every strike, sent waves of power through the air. Skrymir and Fenris, hidden in the shadows, watched in awe, waiting for the right moment to intervene.

With a roar of rage, Bergelmir swung his massive hand at Thor. The blow was so powerful that it sent Thor flying through the air like a severed arrowhead. With a crash, Thor hit the ground next to Skrymir and Fenris, who both recoiled in surprise.

Dust rose around Thor as he tried to rise. His strength was incredible, but Bergelmir's blow had taken the wind out of him.

Thor looked over at Skrymir, who stood astonished, watching the great god.

"If you want to live a little longer, giant, you'd better run with your wolf," Thor said. "We'll meet again another day."

Skrymir looked over at Fenris, who nodded in agreement. "Let's get away," he said.

Thor took a deep breath, stood up, and looked at Bergelmir, who stood triumphantly before them. With Mjolnir tightly gripped in his hand, Thor prepared for the next round in the battle against the mighty mountain.

"Come on, Bergelmir!" Thor shouted with a tone of unshakeable determination. "Can't you handle more?" "You must have slept too long!"

Skrymir and Fenris watched Thor with wonder and admiration as he rose from the ground with Mjolnir in hand, ready for another duel with Bergelmir. Thor, his muscles tense and eyes shining with firm determination, swung Mjolnir in an impressive arc towards Bergelmir.

Skrymir shook his head slightly with a smile. "He is a tireless warrior, that much is certain," he remarked, his deep voice filled with respect. Fenris nodded, his eyes closely following Thor's movements, impressed by his will and strength.

With one last look at the ongoing battle between Thor and Bergelmir, Skrymir and Fenris decided to slip away from the fight with their lives intact.

Skrymir and Fenris hurried through the dense forest, their steps heavy and purposeful. Leaves rustled above them, and the sun's rays cast shifting patterns on the forest floor.
They were now far from the battle but could still hear it and feel it in the wind that whistled through the trees.

But their focus was elsewhere; they were headed to Thorgard's cave to see what had happened to their friends. Had Thor killed them all?

They approached the cave, its entrance becoming increasingly visible through the dense trees. From a distance, one could see that the otherwise beautiful gate that had adorned the cave was torn out and lay in many pieces around the landscape.

As they got closer, they could hear a deep rumbling rolling out from its dark depths. Fenris' ears pricked up, and he growled softly, ready for the unexpected. Skrymir calmly raised his large fist as a sign that they should be on guard.

They looked into the cave, its interior lit by a faint glow that filtered through cracks in the ceiling. Stone formations along the walls cast bizarre shadows, and a cool breeze brushed past them.

Suddenly, they heard a rustle, and a pair of eyes glinted in the darkness. Skrymir and Fenris exchanged a look that reflected their readiness.

From the dark interior of the cave, they were greeted by a familiar figure, an ancient giant whose appearance bore the marks of time.

With a warm smile, the old giant stepped forward, his voice deep and resonant in the cave's silence. "Skrymir, Fenris," he said with a voice that carried tones from the dawn of time. "It's good to see you again." "Where have you been?"

Skrymir and Fenris exchanged a look, a silent agreement between old friends, before Skrymir stepped forward and replied: "We were chased by Thor, how are the giants doing?"

"The giants? Oh, they're not doing very well," exclaimed the old giant. "Come with me, and I'll show you how bad it is."

They walked through the narrow corridors, where one could see marks from lightning on the walls. Past the weapon cabinet, where one could see marks on weapons and shields from the battle against Thor. Skrymir entered the banquet hall, eager to see what awaited him.

They were met by a wave of sound that filled the air with joy and celebration. The sound of giants' laughter and song filled the room, and the scent of food and drink hovered in the air like an enchanted carpet.

The two friends looked around and immediately caught sight of giants sitting around a destroyed long table, laden with feast meals. The large giants laughed and drank, sharing stories and songs that vibrated in the cave walls.

Skrymir and Fenris exchanged a look that said more than a thousand words. They had come to life and celebration and couldn't wait to hear what had happened.

As the party surged in the cave, Skrymir and Fenris suddenly spotted a familiar figure rushing towards them through the crowd. It was Thorgar, the giant king himself. His powerful steps shook the cave floor, and his face lit up in a broad smiling grimace.

Thorgar's dark eyes met Skrymir's and Fenris' gazes with a spark of recognition and joy. His long strides quickly brought him to them, and he stopped right in front of them with an energy that was contagious.

"Welcome back, my friends!" exclaimed Thorgar with a deep, resonant voice that filled the room. "We've been looking for you. How are you?"

He stretched his powerful arms out in a warm embrace that framed them both. After a moment of heartfelt welcome, he stepped back and pointed towards the long table.

"Come, sit down and grab a mug, you look like you have a story," he said with a smile.

Skrymir and Fenris exchanged a look that reflected their earlier battle against Thor. With a bit of reflection, Skrymir replied:

"We were chased through the forest by Thor, and we just managed to escape Thor's wrath. He is a formidable opponent, and we were lucky to get help from a mountain named Bergelmir."

Fenris nodded in agreement and added: "Yes, it was a fight to get away, but we survived and are here now, fortunately."

Thorgar listened attentively and nodded understandingly. "Thor is not to be taken lightly. You have proven your strength and cunning by escaping him. "And Bergelmir, you say? That's a name I didn't think I'd hear again."

Thorgar crossed his arms and began to tell: "Bergelmir is not like other giants. He is one of the oldest giants in Jotunheim, the only one who survived the killing of Ymir.

"The killing of Ymir?" asked Skrymir.

Thorgar leaned over the table "It was a time of chaos and darkness, when the world was shaped by the struggle between fire and ice. Ymir, the first being, was created from melted ice from Niflheim and warm steam from Muspelheim."

"Ymir was enormous, larger than any giant or god, and he was not alone. He soon became the father of a new race, the frost giants. But over time, Ymir became more and more unstable, his violent nature and strength threatening both the gods and the giants."

"It was Odin, Vili, and Ve, the first three Aesir, who decided to act. In a bold move, they killed Ymir. The blood from his body flowed like a river, almost drowning all the frost giants and creating a new world."

Thorgard paused and looked out towards the banquet hall before he began to tell again "Bergelmir and his wife Sifrida were the only ones who survived the great flood that followed. They became the ancestors of the giants, and are the reason we can sit here today."
"You should have seen Bergelmir in his giant form," Thorgard explained, "His figure was impressive, covered in scars and tattoos

that told stories of the many battles he had fought. His hair was long and black as raven feathers, and his eyes glowed like embers from a fire."

"He is known for his strength and his ability to manipulate the elements. Bergelmir has a deep connection to the earth, and he can awaken the mountains and the forest, as you have seen for yourselves. He must have transformed into a mountain. But what truly sets him apart from other giants is his unwavering determination and his unbreakable loyalty to his allies."

"Will he be able to stand against Thor?" asked Skrymir.

Thorgar took a deep breath before continuing, "Battling Bergelmir is like battling the Earth itself. His strength is both impressive and fearsome. He is not a giant one would want to anger unless prepared for a fight of epic proportions. It could go either way."

"However, he hasn't been seen since his wife's death, so he might be a bit rusty if he's been lying dormant for centuries," Thorgar chuckled.

"We should have helped him," Skrymir exclaimed, and Fenris nodded.

"You would have just gotten in the way, like flies among giants," Thorgard said with a laugh. "A battle between Thor and Bergelmir is something to be observed from a distance," Thorgar chuckled again.

"But how did you overcome Thor after he entered the cave?" Skrymir asked.

"We didn't," Thorgard said, pointing towards Grid. "She did."

"Did Grid?" exclaimed Skrymir. "But how?"

"You'll have to ask her, but she did it with her bare hands," Thorgard replied.

Skrymir and Fenris looked astonished, then ran to Grid for an explanation.

"How did you defeat Thor?" Skrymer and Fenris shouted simultaneously.

Grid laughed while stirring the large pots.

"Well, you see," she began, "I was here stirring the pots when suddenly there was a commotion of giants running all over for mead. Then there was a loud bang from the gate. Thor shouted that we should give him the potion of the dead, or he would come in and take it. We didn't have it, so we couldn't give it to him. He started banging on the gate with Mjolnir. Each time the hammer struck the door, it echoed like thunder through the cave. He shouted and threatened, but the gate held."

She chuckled a bit, "I've never seen anyone so obsessed with getting into our cave."

"It would have held if it weren't for the peephole in the door. Thor sent lightning into the entrance, and the gate burst from within. I've told Thorgard many times that the peephole was a bad idea, but he wanted to see who was coming."

Grid stopped stirring the pot. "All the giants in the narrow corridor were thrown into the common hall by a huge bolt of lightning. And then Thor stepped in."

"I remember it clearly," she began, "When Thor, with his powerful body and his characteristic beard, entered the hall. His eyes quickly scanned the room, and with each step he took, the hall echoed with the sound of his heavy footsteps."

She continued to describe Thor's imposing figure, his hair pulled back in a tight bun, and how even without Mjolnir, his mighty hammer, he was a fearsome sight. Grid's voice was filled with respect as she described Thor's presence and the intense atmosphere that filled the room.

"Thor took a deep breath," Grid continued, "and lifted his head, his eyes locked on Thorgar at the end of the hall. A quiet murmur went through the crowd as they waited for what would happen next."

They all prepared to rush towards Thor. "Then he grabbed the long table and swung it, piling everyone on top of each other," she laughed.

"Then I could see from behind that his gloves were damaged. So when he asked again where the eternal potion of death was, I got an idea."

"I told him I knew where it was, and if he could hold the pot at arm's length longer than me, I would tell him. But if not, he would have to leave this cave."

He just laughed and said, "a simple giantess cannot match a god," and accepted the challenge.

So there we stood, each with our pot. "What Thor didn't know is that these are magical pots, forged by an ancient giant, heated directly from Helheim, making them impossible to hold without magical gloves," she explained, showing off the gloves she wore.

Skrymir stared intently at the gloves. Grid's magical gloves were made from the finest, strongest leather from the deep forests of Jotunheim, reinforced with small inlaid plates of silver and gold, beautifully carved with patterns of runes and magical symbols. Each finger was highlighted with a different color, representing the various powers the gloves could channel.

When Grid wore these gloves, her fingers were enveloped in a faint, shimmering aura. With a simple movement, she could channel and control the elements she desired. The gloves enhanced her abilities, allowing her to cast stronger spells, create powerful energy beams, or protect herself and others with magical shields.

You should have been here! Here I stood, little Grid, facing Thor. Two giant pots stood between us, their steam filling the air with the intense heat from Helheim.

"Are you ready, Thor?" I asked, my eyes meeting his.

"He nodded confidently and lifted his pot with effort. I took a deep breath, grasped my pot, and lifted it with a firmness that could only come from centuries of training with these gloves. Helheim's heat tried to penetrate, but my gloves kept it at bay."

"As time passed, it became increasingly clear that Thor was struggling. His breathing became heavier, and his face turned red with effort. I could see his grip starting to fail, and the pot began to slip from his hands."

"I stood firm as a rock. As my eyes met Thor's, I could sense infinite pain in those otherwise tough eyes. After what felt like an eternity but was only minutes, Thor had to give up. With a roar of frustration, he dropped his pot, which fell to the ground with a resounding crash."

"I told him about the magical pots and how my gloves have protected me from Helheim's fire for decades," "He looked surprised and muttered something about his damaged gloves."

"Looks like I win this round," I said. Thor looked down at his pot, his face a mix of wonder and admiration.

"Thor, although clearly disappointed, nodded in recognition and then walked out of the cave," Grid proudly recounted.

"Wow," exclaimed Skrymir. "To think you defeated Thor with your cunning."

Grid laughed, "Yes, you could say that."

In the back of the cave, where the party was in full swing, Thorgar's powerful voice cut through the noise. "Skrymir!" he shouted with a deep, resonant tone that immediately captured everyone's attention.

Skrymir looked up, having just taken a sip of his drink. His eyes met Thorgar's, and he could see that Thorgar wanted his company. With a slight nod to the giants he was sitting with, Skrymir stood up and stepped out from the shadowy corner where he had been sitting.

He walked through the crowd of partying giants, who respectfully made way for him. When he reached Thorgar's table, he bowed slightly and said, "What can I do for you, Thorgar?"

Thorgar smiled, his eyes twinkling with anticipation. "Skrymir, we need your help," he began, "but first, take a seat and share a drink with me."

With a respectful demeanor, Skrymir sat down beside Thorgar, ready to hear what the elder giant king had in mind.

"As you've seen, we need a new gate, and you need your axe repaired," said Thorgar, swinging a mug of mead. "So here's this lump of gold. Dwarves love gold. Find a dwarf who can build a Thor-stopper."

Skrymir nodded happily, "Thank you, Thorgar," he said.

Chapter 12: Did he die?

The next morning, Skrymir and Fenris set out to find the dwarves. They ventured into the dense, dark forest where branches twisted like long, shadowy arms through the thick foliage.

"Do you think he's still alive?" Fenris asked with a deep, resonant voice that almost rose above the forest's whisper.

"I don't know," Skrymir replied.

Skrymir looked around, his eyes searching for signs of Bergelmir's presence. "If he is alive, the forest will tell us," he said, listening to the distant sounds of wildlife and the wind rustling through the trees like whispering tales.

They continued through the forest, ready for whatever they might encounter. After hours of walking, they reached a large clearing.

Skrymir looked towards the horizon where the peak of Bergelmir was usually visible. "Let's see," he said.

After several more hours of walking, the forest opened up, and they stood at the base of what once was the mighty Bergelmir Mountain. Now, it was reduced to a large pile of rocks and stones scattered around, like the remnants of a once proud creature.

Skrymir and Fenris stood still for a moment, overwhelmed by the sight. "So Thor has truly defeated him," Fenris muttered, his voice filled with a mix of respect and awe.

Skrymir nodded, his gaze fixed on the shattered remains of the mountain. "Yes, it appears so. Thor has demonstrated his strength here."

They slowly walked through the crushed rocks and stones, treading carefully not to disturb the site where Bergelmir once stood. Although the mountain's physical form had changed, they could still feel the old giant's presence in the air, a sense of strength and ancient wisdom.

Bergelmir's eyes slowly opened, and he looked down at them with a deep, rolling laugh. "If you've also come to fight, I have more to offer," he said with a deep voice that shook the ground beneath them.

Skrymir and Fenris exchanged a quick glance before stepping forward and greeting Bergelmir with the respect such an ancient and mighty being deserved.

"We haven't come to harm you; we've come to take you back to the cave with the other giants," Skrymir shouted to Bergelmir.

Bergelmir laughed again, a deep, booming laugh that filled the forest. "Fear not for me, young giant. It takes more to defeat me. I have found peace here in the forest, and here I will stay."

After a moment of silence, Bergelmir said, "Ever since my wife was captured in Helheim, I just wanted to be here."

"Captured?" Fenris asked.

"I probably shouldn't say this, but she was captured in Helheim by the goddess Hel. There she must stay forever."

"Why was she captured?" Fenris asked again.

"I promised the gods not to tell, but the gods are afraid that a very special potion might fall into the wrong hands."

Fenris and Skrymir looked at Bergelmir in astonishment as he continued.

"Ymir, one of the first giants, received a magical potion from an ancient wizard. This potion contained some of the substances used in the creation of the nine worlds."

"When he drank it, he grew and grew, and he couldn't stop drinking it. Eventually, he was so large that there was no longer room for him. You should have seen him," laughed Bergelmir.

"Ymir was a being of unimaginable size," Bergelmir began, letting his eyes wander across the horizon. "His body stretched as far as the eye could see, and his strength was unmatched among the giants."

"He was like a living mountain range, whose shadow cast darkness over the entire world. His breath created winds, and his footsteps shaped valleys. He was the beginning of everything, and his body carried powers that even the gods had to respect."

"But with greatness also came danger," Bergelmir continued, a touch of seriousness in his voice. "For Ymir was not only a creator but also a destroyer. His power was unstoppable, and he could crush anything in his path."

"The potion had a downside; his mind grew darker and darker, and eventually, he challenged the gods to battle," Bergelmir's voice now carried a hint of sadness. "Odin killed Ymir while he was sleeping."

"I curse that potion. Why did Ymir also have to tell me who had made that potion?" Bergelmir looked lost in thought. "The gods were afraid I would seek revenge for Ymir's death or reveal who had made the potion, so they imprisoned my wife in Helheim."

"That's why I transformed myself into a mountain, so the gods can see that I am no threat, and hopefully, they will set my wife free."

"Why didn't they just imprison you?" Fenris asked. "Who knows what those gods think sometimes, maybe they were afraid I would tell hell."

"May I hear about the fight against Thor?" Skrymir interrupted.

Bergelmir's eyes lit up, "The fight against Thor, yes, that was quite a battle."

Thor and I stood facing each other, standing like two titans in the heat of battle. Thor, with his mighty hammer Mjolnir, which had already defeated so many of my giant brothers.

The clouds gathered above us, and the wind howled through the trees, as if nature itself knew what was coming. Thor raised Mjolnir, its glowing power lighting up in his eyes, ready for battle.

"We collided with tremendous force, mountain against hammer. I fought with everything I had, Thor's blows were quick and powerful. Each time Mjolnir struck, the earth shook beneath my feet, and rock fragments flew around."

"The battle ended when I landed a blow on him, and as he flew back, he threw Mjolnir, which shattered my left arm. When the hammer flew back again, he didn't catch it. It simply fell out of his hand; I've never seen anything like it. So I seized the opportunity and lunged at him with all I had."

"Unfortunately, the hammer swung over to one of his foolish goats, which swung the hammer back to him with its antlers."

"With my entire left side exposed, and in the process of striking him with my right, he landed a blow so hard on my head that all of Jotunheim shook."

When the dust settled, Thor stood there as the victor. He looked tired but satisfied, his gaze met mine, and I could see respect in his eyes, but also an unyielding determination.

"You fought well, Bergelmir," he said, panting and sweating from the battle.

Although I had lost, I felt a deep respect for Thor and his strength. Before he flew on his goats, he said I should stop by Midgard to see all the glory that Ymir had created.

"Did Ymir create Midgard?" Fenris asked.

"You could say that," Bergelmir said. After they had killed Ymir, they made Midgard from his body. There was so much blood that everyone I knew drowned. "I barely escaped by sailing around in Ymir's heart."

"The gods are insane; they must be stopped," Skrymir exclaimed.

Bergelmir looked at Skrymir and laughed, "If only it were that easy, little giant. Many have tried."

Skrymir straightened up and said, "When the dwarves fix my axe, I'll teach those gods that you can't just kill people." Bergelmir laughed again. "If you're going to the dwarves, good luck getting them to make anything."

"If you're lucky, I have a gift for you; it's a piece of Ymir's heart, it might give your weapon strength and courage."

A rock opened, and there lay a piece of the heart, which over time had turned into a dark red diamond. Skrymir picked it up, looking amazed at it. It was as if the universe was hidden in the stone; it sparkled and glittered, looking like there were billions of tiny suns.

"Thank you, Bergelmir," expressed Skrymir.

"It was nothing, now get going. I need 100,000 years to become a mountain again, can't waste my time standing and talking."

Skrymir and Fenris laughed and began walking away from Bergelmir towards the home of the dwarves.

Chapter 13: The World of Dwarves

Skrymir and Fenris walked through the dense forests of Jotunheim, bathed in deep moonlight. The sound of their heavy footsteps subdued the surroundings as they carefully treaded to avoid awakening the forest dwellers.

The dwarves' cave was only a day's journey away, a place everyone had heard of but no one visited. Giants were not pleased with how the dwarves dug and chopped at nature, preferring to live in harmony with it instead. However, they tolerated the dwarves because they needed the precious stones and metals for their magic.

As Fenris and Skrymir approached the dwarves' cave, they sensed the heavy scent of earth and stone filling the air. The sound of picks striking rocks and ore carts pulled by sturdy ponies echoed from afar.

The cave entrance was wide and dark, framed by steep cliffs that seemed to guard the entrance. Inside, a labyrinth of tunnels was illuminated by the glow of fires and glowing lamps hanging from the ceiling.

They were greeted by an old dwarf at the entrance, who asked if they came to trade and if they brought payment. Skrymir nodded and showed him the gold nugget he had received from Thorgard. The dwarf beckoned them to follow him deeper into the cave.

The dwarves, clad in rough garments and dirty faces, tirelessly worked on their crafts. Some forged weapons and jewelry, while others mined minerals and gemstones from deep within.

Fenris and Skrymir met the dwarven leader, an older dwarf with a face covered in beard and sparkling eyes. He welcomed them with a deep, rumbling voice and led them through the busy corridors to a place where they could rest after their long journey. He showed them a sleeping area and a spot by a fire where they could eat, then left them to themselves.

As they sat by the fire, surrounded by the buzz of dwarven activity, they felt the tense energy that filled the place. It was clear that this was a site of great importance to the dwarves, where their skills and craftsmanship were highly valued and fully utilized.

Skrymir called out to a dwarf, "Hey, you, can you help us?"

"If it's a bet, I'm not betting," replied the dwarf. "No, not betting, just need to know who to talk to," Skrymir responded.

"Talk to? I'm no snitch!" the dwarf retorted.

"No, if I need an axe repaired, who can help with that?"

"Ahh, depends on the axe, may I see it?"

Skrymir presented the axe head and broken handle.

The dwarf took the axe head and examined it intently. "Hmm, this axe is made in Nidavellir, you won't find a dwarf here willing to repair it."

"Nidavellir?" asked Fenris.

"That's the world of dwarves, filled with dwarves who are snobbish and think they can do everything. Ever since Sindri and Brokkr made Mjolnir, they've felt superior to us other dwarves. But we have dwarves here who could craft something much better than Mjolnir."

"Better than Mjolnir? I doubt that, I bet you can't make a gate for the giants' cave that can withstand Mjolnir," said Skrymir.

"How dare you, we easily can!" the dwarf replied.

"Prove it, we bet this gold nugget that you can't make a gate that withstands Mjolnir."

The dwarf eyed the gold nugget hungrily. "HA, you're on!" he exclaimed.

Skrymir tossed the gold nugget to him, and the dwarf looked back in astonishment. "Alright, if there's no gate when I return to the giants' cave, Fenris will come to collect the gold nugget, and by then he'll be twice as big!"

The dwarf looked up from the gold nugget, "It's a deal," he said.

"How do we get to Nidavellir?" asked Skrymir.

"There's a portal, but I'm not sure if it can fit a giant and a wolf, or if it's just for dwarves. We can ask a dwarf named Alvis, he's the wisest I know."

"Follow me," said the dwarf, rising from the fireside. He led them deeper into the cave, and Fenris and Skrymir followed.

Skrymir and Fenris delved deeper into the dwarven cave, stretching into the darkness like an endless abyss. They could hear the sound of dwarven hammers forging and clanging on metal deep within the caverns. With each step into the cave, the air grew thicker with the scent of metal and the echoing clangs of dwarven labor.

They moved cautiously through the winding corridors, lit by sparse lamps casting ghostly shadows on the walls. Skrymir's large strides thundered in the dim space, while Fenris' eyes glowed with excitement.

In a clearing, Alvis stood with a sly smile as he saw them. Alvis was a dwarf of impressive stature, even for a dwarf, his face marked by a life filled with wisdom and experience. Despite his short height, Alvis radiated an aura of authority and confidence, and his voice carried the tone of ancient secrets and wise words. He wore garments of animal skins and iron fittings, and his brown eyes twinkled with an understanding of the world around him that few possessed.

"Welcome, great giant with wolf," said Alvis with a twinkle in his eye. "What can I assist you with?"

"We wish to get to Nidavellir," said Fenris, "Can you help us?"

"Nidavellir," exclaimed Alvis, "It's difficult to get a giant and wolf into Nidavellir, but it can be done. If you answer my questions correctly, I will help you. But if you answer incorrectly, you must help me."

Skrymir and Fenris nodded eagerly and prepared to answer Alvis' questions.

"The first question," said Alvis, "What is the name of the mighty river that flows through Jotunheim?"

Skrymir thought quickly and answered: "It is Elivagar, the mighty river, which springs from the world tree Yggdrasil itself."

Alvis nodded approvingly and continued: "The next question: How many mountain ranges surround Jotunheim?"

Skrymir gazed into the distance and answered: "Jotunheim is surrounded by seven mighty mountain ranges, standing as guardians over our realm."

Alvis smiled broadly and posed the last question: "What is the name of the legendary giant king said to have built the first fortresses in Jotunheim?"

Skrymir did not hesitate and proudly replied: "It is Thrym, the great and mighty king, who ruled our realm with wisdom and strength."

Alvis clapped excitedly and declared Skrymir and Fenris winners of the challenge. Alvis then explained that they just needed to go through the portal, and where they could find the portal.

Skrymir thanked him for the help, and they continued through the cave towards the portal.

As they approached the portal to Nidavellir, they felt an intense heat streaming out through the cracks. The dwarven home was known for its forges, creating the most magical and powerful items in all nine worlds.

Suddenly, they stood before the portal, a massive door of gilded steel, engraved with intricate patterns and rune inscriptions. Skrymir and Fenris exchanged a look filled with anticipation, well aware that behind this door lay a treasure trove of endless riches and secrets. With a great effort, Skrymir opened the door, and a wave of heat and light streamed out.

Before they entered the portal, Skrymir looked over at the dwarf who had helped them find the door.

"Thanks for the help, what's your name?"

"Andvare," replied the dwarf.

Skrymir nodded appreciatively and stepped through the portal with Fenris right behind him.
Many had heard legendary tales of the dwarven realm, where skilled artisans shaped metals and gemstones into the most enchanting artworks.

They stepped out of the gate to Nidavellir, revealing a massive stone structure behind them, covered in ancient runes and engraved symbols. A sense of awe overwhelmed them as they admired its impressive facade, which seemed to recount tales of past grandeur and the magic of craftsmanship.

With hearts pounding in anticipation, they proceeded through a corridor leading them up and into the inner sanctum of Nidavellir.

Immediately, they were embraced by a world of wondrous mines and stone caverns, illuminated by sparkling gemstones and the soft glow of faint light sources. The sound of dynamic tools and blacksmithing filled the air, and they watched the dwarves at work, each deeply engrossed in their craft.

"So, here we are, Fenris. Who do you think can make the axe?" asked Skrymir.

"We could try asking Sindri and Brokkr. If they can make Mjolnir, they can probably fix the axe," replied Fenris.

"Good idea, let's try to find them," Skrymir said with a smile.

Through dim passages and glittering mines, Fenris and Skrymir made their way, their footsteps echoing against the raw stone walls of the dwarven realm. A trail of golden tracks led them deeper into this subterranean labyrinth, where a treasury of craftsmanship and artistic splendor awaited discovery.

They asked random dwarves along the way and were directed deeper into Nidavellir until they reached an elevated space where a luminous cave revealed itself. It was here, deep within Nidavellir, that they hoped to find the dwarves Sindri and Brokkr, masters of metallurgy and blacksmithing.

As they entered the impressive hall, they were greeted by a

symphony of hammers meeting metal in a feverish dance of craftsmanship. Rows of sculptures and gleaming weapons adorned the room's walls, and a warm glow from the smiths' forges cast a golden hue over everything.

Amidst this noise of activity, the two giants spotted a pair of dwarves, surrounded by a crowd of apprentices and helpers. Sindri, with his crooked smile and sparkling eyes, worked with unstoppable energy, while Brokkr, with his powerful hand, shaped metal with almost supernatural precision.

With respectful steps, Skrymir and Fenris approached Sindri and Brokkr, who were deeply absorbed in their work. The two giants waited patiently until the dwarves looked up and met their intense gazes.

"Honored masters of Nidavellir," Skrymir began, his voice filled with awe, "we come to you with a humble request for help."

Brokkr and Sindri looked up from their work, curiosity sparkling in their eyes.

"My axe," continued Skrymir, lifting the massive weapon, "has been damaged in our recent battle. We have heard of your unparalleled craftsmanship and hope you can help us repair it."

The dwarves exchanged a knowing glance.

"We will do our best to assist you," said Sindri, his voice carrying traces of confidence and experience. "Let's examine the axe and assess the damage."

They took the axe to a well-lit corner of the forge, where they could inspect the damage in detail. The smiths' expert eyes studied every crack and bend as they eagerly discussed potential solutions.

After a brief evaluation, Sindri and Brokkr nodded to each other with assurance before turning to the giants with a smile. "We can help you, but it will cost," declared Brokkr. "It's an old axe, with old magic."

"Cost?" exclaimed Skrymir. "Isn't it just a matter of hammering it a bit? Why should you charge for that?"

"We no longer work for giants for free, especially after the last giant here cheated us," Sindri retorted.

"Who cheated you?" asked Skrymir.

"My brother Brokkr and I were challenged by the cunning Loki," Sindri began, sitting by the forge. "Loki claimed that we dwarf smiths could never match our past masterpieces. It deeply challenged us, and we decided to prove him wrong."

"He told us that if we won, we could have his head. Who could say no to that?" laughed Brokkr.

With intense concentration, Sindri continued, "I immediately began forging the shaft of Gungnir, the legendary spear that would never miss its target. I used the finest iron I could find and added secret enchantments to make it invincible."

"Meanwhile, my brother Brokkr started forging Draupnir, a magical gold ring that had the ability to replicate itself, creating eight other rings every ninth night," added Sindri proudly.

"During our work, Loki tried to disrupt us by transforming into a fly to bother me, but I remained focused and still managed to forge Gungnir's shaft. Brokkr was also challenged by Loki's tricks; he bit him on the neck! However, he managed to complete Draupnir despite this," Sindri explained.

"But when we were about to make Mjolnir, he poked me in the eye. I couldn't see afterward and made my first and biggest mistake. The handle was too short."

As he concluded the story, Sindri smiled at Skrymir and Fenris. "However, we did sew the annoying giant's mouth shut. We would have taken his entire head, but he tricked us." "So you can see, we can't just fix your axe; you could be Loki in disguise."

"That makes sense," said Skrymir, "but we have nothing to pay with; Andvari has taken all our gold."

"HA. Have you given all your gold to Andvari? I hope you didn't need to buy anything, for he only collects for his treasure," Brokkr exclaimed.

Skrymir looked worriedly at Fenris. "Do you want to ask Andvari if he has made the gate?"

Fenris nodded and said goodbye before leaving the dwarven workshop.

Fenris purposefully made his way through Nidavellir, through the narrow corridors towards the gate to Jotunheim. The dwarves turned their heads as he passed, for it was not every day that a great wolf walked alone through their city.

"You shouldn't worry; Andvari just loves treasures but is honest enough," Brokkr said to Skrymir. "Do you want to come down and play some dice?"

"Dice?" "I've never tried that before."

"Then you should definitely try it; it's fun and keeps the mind sharp." "Come on," said Brokkr.

They walked out of the workshop together, and Skrymir followed the dwarf through the corridors to the outskirts of Nidavellir.

Meanwhile, Fenris had passed through the gate and was now in the dwarven cave in Jotunheim again. He wondered where he would find Andvari as he trotted through their cave.

Skrymir and Brokkr had arrived at a small door with a sign above it reading Nida's Tavern. It was a small inn from the giants' perspective, but laughter could be heard behind the door. Brokkr opened the door with a smile and gestured for Skrymir to follow.

Skrymir entered the dwarven tavern with Brokkr and was immediately greeted by the rustic and cozy atmosphere characteristic of dwarven meeting places.

The room was low-ceilinged and lit by flickering torches that cast warm, golden tones over the roughly hewn stone walls. Wisps of smoke hovered in the air, mixing with the scent of freshly brewed beer and roasted tubers served at the bar.

Along the walls were heavy wooden tables and benches where dwarves gathered in groups, laughing and talking loudly as they enjoyed their beverages and shared stories of their latest adventures and mining feats. A few of the tables were occupied by intense dice games, with dwarves throwing the dice with enthusiasm and laughter.

At one end of the tavern was a large open fireplace, where flames crackled and cast a warm glow into the room, and a couple of cozy armchairs were pulled close to the warmth.

Behind the bar stood a robust dwarf with a broad smile, serving drinks and snacks to the thirsty and hungry patrons. The shelves behind him were filled with bottles of various strong drinks and jars of homemade honey wine and other specialties.

It was a place filled with life, warmth, and community, where dwarves could relax after a hard day in the mines or prepare for their next adventure in the endless mountains and underground passages.

"Ha! Got more to say?" shouted from the bar. Brokkr laughed and walked up to the bar with Skrymir.

As they approached, Brokkr handed a gold coin to Skrymir. "Here, you can borrow this so you can join the tournament."

Skrymir nodded and smiled before they reached the bar.

"Two large mugs of mead, and we'd like to join the tournament," said Brokkr.
'So gladly,' said the dwarf behind the bar, filling two mugs as big as her head.

'Have you played before?' she asked Skrymir, who stood looking puzzled.

'No,' said Skrymir.

'That's so typical of you, Brokkr, inviting someone without telling the rules,' said the dwarf behind the bar.

'What's your name?'

'Skrymir.'

- 'Each of us will use five dice, Skrymir. And a mug to hide them during the round.'

- 'The goal is to guess how many dice with a certain value, that everyone has, Skrymir.'

1. 'First, we roll the dice, Skrymir, but we must keep the results hidden from each other.'
2. 'After we look at our dice, we guess how many dice show a specific value in total. For example, how many dice show a '6'.'
3. 'The first time, I will say my guess aloud, so you hear it, Skrymir. For example: 'There are at least three sixes in total.''
4. 'Now it's your turn, Skrymir. You can increase the number of the challenged dice value or say that I am lying.'
5. 'If you challenge my guess, we reveal all the dice. If there aren't as many sixes as I said, you lose a die. But if there are, I lose a die.'
6. 'We take turns like this, until only one of us is left with dice.'

'The last of us with dice remaining, wins.'
There you go, Skyrmr, now you're ready to play!

Skyrmir thanked him and joined Brokkr at a table where eight other dwarves were seated. A larger chair was brought forward, and Skyrmir was given a mug with dice that were much bigger than those of the other dwarves.

The game would start soon, one of the dwarves mentioned. So, he simply sat and listened to the dwarves' conversations, usually about what they had been working on in their workshops or in the mines."

Chapter 14: The contest

Fenris padded around the dwarves' cave, searching for Andvare, but to no avail. He asked various dwarves if they had seen him, until an old dwarf mentioned that Andvare usually hung out by the river.

Thus, Fenris continued out of the cave and followed the path down to the river. He felt a surge of excitement in his chest. The thought of finding Andvare so that Skrymir could have his axe repaired filled him with joy.

The path meandered through the dense forest, and soon the roaring sound of the river broke through the silence. The noise of water rushing against stones guided Fenris closer. He stepped toward the riverbank, where the water flowed clear and cold from the mountains.

On the opposite bank, nestled in a small green slope, sat a dwarf. His beard was as gray as the mountain stones, and his eyes sparkled like diamonds in the sunlight. When he saw Fenris, he stood up and met his gaze with a curious raise of his eyebrows.

"Fenris? I've heard of you," said the dwarf, his voice carrying centuries of wisdom. "My name is Odder. Welcome to my beloved river. What brings you here?"

Fenris moved closer, his paws against the cool stones. "I'm looking for Andvare," he stated firmly. "I need his advice and wisdom."

The dwarf nodded understandingly and pointed across the river. "Andvare stays over there, by the riverbank. I can guide you there, but only if you beat me in a race."

"Beat you in a race?" Fenris asked.

"Yes, a wolf like you should be much faster than an old dwarf like me."

"Alright, what shall we compete in?" Fenris inquired.

"We shall swim across the river," Odder declared.

"Hmm. I'm not sure what you're up to, dwarf, but I accept!" Fenris thought it would be easy.

Fenris stood by the river's edge, looking out over the clear, flowing water. He felt the excitement build in his chest as he prepared for the challenging race against Odder.

He glanced at Odder, who wore a broad smile. Suddenly, with a puff, Odder disappeared, and in his place was an otter. Odder had transformed into his namesake.

"Hey, that's cheating!" exclaimed Fenris.

"You should have said no transformations were allowed," laughed Odder, diving into the water.

With a deep breath, Fenris plunged into the river and began to swim with powerful strokes. The water yielded under his strong movements, and he sliced through it with almost supernatural ease.

Beside him, he suddenly saw a figure emerge from the water. It was Odder, whose agile movements and quick pace even surprised Fenris. He knew this would not be an easy match.

Odder swam with playful elegance, as if dancing with the currents. Fenris tried to keep up with his swift movements, but Odder was fast. He cut through the water like an arrow, moving with an effortless grace.

Despite Fenris's best efforts, it was clear that Odder was superior. He transformed into a shadow on the water, quickly pulling ahead of Fenris and nearing victory with every wave-like stroke.

Eventually, when Odder reached the riverbank first, he climbed onto the shore and turned triumphantly toward Fenris. Although Fenris had fought with all his might, it was clear that Odder was the rightful winner of the race.

Fenris took a deep breath and looked at Odder with respect. He had faced a worthy opponent and now had to accept his defeat.

"Well swum, cunning dwarf, but wait, we didn't wager anything if you won?" Fenris remarked.

Odder chuckled and replied, "No, wouldn't want to upset a wolf, just thought it would be fun to race."

"If you just help me and my friend Alvis drink a bit from Mimer's well, then I'll help you find Andvare," Odder proposed.

"Mimer's well?" Fenris asked curiously.

"Yes, Mimer's well, nothing you need to worry about."

"Why not just drink from the lake?" Fenris wondered aloud.

"Come on, Mimer lives right over here," Odder said, pointing.

They walked over to Mimer's home, which was situated next to a tree, the largest Fenris had ever seen. He paused, looking up at the impressive tree.

"Yes, it's a beautiful tree, visible from all over Jotunheim," Odder told Fenris, waving to Alvis, a dwarf standing by the tree.

Fenris nodded, "Ah, that was what I saw on the horizon."

"That's Mimer's tree. My plan is for you and Alvis to cut it down, and when it falls, we'll run in and drink from his well. Make sure it falls towards Elvigar, so no one gets hurt."

Alvis greeted Fenris, and just then, with a puff, Alvis transformed into a beaver.

"This day keeps getting weirder," Fenris exclaimed.

Alvis explained, "I was cursed by a Norn once for cutting down one of their sacred trees, so whenever there's sunlight, I turn into a beaver. I think if I drink a bit from Mimer's well, I'll become wise and worthy of being with Trud, my beloved."

"Wise? What's with the well, and won't Mimer be mad if we cut down his tree?" Fenris asked.

"Probably, but the tree is connected to a well he guards and only allows the chosen to drink from," Odder replied seriously. "It's the well of wisdom, where all the world's secrets and treasures are kept."

"He's in league with Odin," Alvis added. "He helps him with wisdom and even let him drink from the well in exchange for an eye. That's why it's good if we cut down the tree."

"That must have been what made him cunning enough to trick Suttung. Let's cut down that tree," Fenris said, and together with Alvis, they began to bite into the tree. Meanwhile, the dwarves had finally begun to play dice. Skrymir was drowsy after sitting and listening to the dwarves for so long, but now the dice were thrown.

The atmosphere grew intense, and anticipation hung thick in the air as they threw their first dice.

Skrymir threw his dice and looked into his cup. They all had 5 dice, so he had to predict how many eyes were among the 8 players and guess higher than the previous dwarf. The dwarf before him said there were 15 fives. Skrymir thought that was set very low, but they were just starting. He looked at his dice again; there were 3 sixes, 1 four, and 1 three, so he said 15 sixes.

"Hmm," he said, "then there must also be 16 sixes."

Rounds went quickly, and the tension built as each participant tried to predict each other's moves and decipher the hidden intentions behind their actions. The dwarves shouted and laughed as they challenged each other in this game of skill and deception.

Skrymir, with his roguish smile, threw the dice with confidence, trying to trick his opponents with false guesses and strategic bluffs. He guessed that his opponents had higher results, even when he knew it wasn't the case, and he exploited their trust to gain an advantage.

However, the other dwarves were not easy to fool. They were experienced players and quick to reveal Skrymir's deceit. They guessed he was bluffing when he claimed to have a higher combination, and they exploited his weaknesses to their advantage.

Skrymir noticed that the more the dwarves drank, the more they lied about the result of their dice. So he took advantage of being three times their size and often fetched new mugs of mead to the table.

After a long time, he was now alone with the last dwarf, and they each had 1 die left. It was Skrymir's turn to go first.

He looked under his mug at what the die showed. It was a four. He thought about what to say. Skrymir looked at the dwarf, who sat half-drunk with a smile.

He looked down at the die and then said there was one five. The dwarf looked at his die and then looked up at Skrymir. The dwarf said there was one six.

Skrymir thought about it. Should he say 2 fives? Should he believe the dwarf had one six? Skrymir was about to say 2 fives when suddenly there was a jolt in his chest. Everything dangled and spun, and it felt like there was great danger on the way. What was that feeling, and where did it come from? Meanwhile, Fenris was busy gnawing on the tree with his new friends Odder and Alvis when a tall, slender figure in a dark shape stepped forward.

"What are you doing?" he asked loudly.

Fenris was shocked, so he jumped up the tree and clung to it, slowly sliding down again with his claws in the tree while he looked around at the stranger.

Fenris had never seen anyone like him. With red hair that sparkled like sparks from a fire, and his eyes that glowed like embers in the dark, he was a figure of both enchantment and danger. His agile movements reminded Fenris of a cunning fox lurking in the deep undergrowth, always ready to sneak in and trick his prey. "A wolf, a beaver, and an otter," said the figure. "I don't know what you look like."

Alvis stepped forward. "I am a beaver, it is in my nature to fell trees, how dare you disturb my work."

Odder pointed at the figure, "haven't I seen you before, you seem familiar?" step closer, my eyes are better in water.

The figure stepped closer, "Shut up, you ugly otter, I'm not here for an ugly animal like you, but for you, Fenris."

"How do you know my name?" Fenris asked.

"It was I who gave you the name when you ran around in my world," the figure replied.

"Do you know me?" Fenris replied curiously.

"I know you all too well," "That's why I also know what you can become, and therefore I must unfortunately kill you," "I would have liked to see you grow up, but unfortunately I have orders from higher powers."

Fenris growled and took a step forward. "We are not afraid," he said in a dark tone.

The figure laughed and shook his head. "Good to hear." "But remember, not everything is as it seems."

Suddenly there was a deep rumble from the forest, Odder, Alvis, and Fenris exchanged worried glances. "We must get away," said Odder quickly. "Come, Fenris." As they jumped onto his back.

The three turned around and ran towards the forest, while the figure stood back and watched them with a cold smile. "Hate to run, good thing I'm so good at throwing," he muttered to himself as he picked up a stone.

He aimed at Fenris, who ran as fast as he could with Odder and Alvis on his back.

With a hard swing, there was a sound through the trees from the stone, which flew through the air at high speed.

Bang, it said, and the stone had hit right in the temple, and down he fell flat on the ground. The eyes were extinguished, and life slowly left the body.

Meanwhile, Skrymir was about to lift his mug, still with the strange feeling in his body. He lifted the mug, and so did the dwarf. The dwarf had one three, so Skrymir won.

The gold was his, he thought about the strange feeling, and was amazed that he apparently had a sixth sense that could sense danger. Will he ever lose at dice again if he is warned before he can lose?

In front of him, there was now a large pile of gold, and full dwarves, who sang and half-slept around him. Skrymir looked down at his mead, why did he have such a strange feeling in his stomach, as if he was going to throw up?

Skrymir sat and thought. "Could there be something wrong with the mead, shouldn't I be having fun, and I've earned a lot of gold." "Enough to get both the axe and the gate repaired." "Must be because I'm missing something to eat."

Skrymir went up to the bar to order some food, on the way up he was met by a dwarf who asked if he would like to play stone throw. That could be fun, Skrymir replied.

Meanwhile, Fenris and Alvis had stopped after Odder fell lifelessly down from Fenris' back, he had been hit by the stone right in the temple. There he lay now, transformed back into a dwarf. Alvis slapped him on the cheeks with his tail, trying to wake him up.

Meanwhile, Fenris had taken a position in front of Odder, ready to take on the figure. He looked at the figure, his agile movements reminiscent of a cunning fox lurking in the deep, always ready to sneak in and trick his prey.

The figure laughed, "How can I hit the little one when there was something so big right below" "Must be because I'm not done playing with you, Fenris"

"You don't touch Odder!" Fenris shouted.

"Odder you say, and that's not an otter lying there, it's a dwarf," the figure replied. "Could it be Redmir's son Odder?"

"Yes, and you won't get past me, I'll kill you," Alvis shouted followed by a little growl.

The figure now walked quickly towards Fenris.

Fenris was about to bite, but with a quick blow from the figure, he was thrown to the side.

"Fuck, Fuck, Fuck" "What have I done," exclaimed the figure and held his head. "Hope he's not dead!!" No, no, no.

The figure pushed Alvis aside, who had jumped at him with his teeth first. Then he picked up Odder and disappeared with a puff.

Meanwhile, the strange feeling had disappeared from Skrymir's body. It must be the food, he thought to himself. Let's win some more gold in Stone Throw.

Skrymir and the dwarf stood facing each other, their eyes gleaming with a competitive spirit. The first round began, and Skrymir grabbed a heavy stone from the pile. With a powerful swing of his arm, he sent the stone flying, and it landed close to the target, and Skrymir was met with an approving nod from his opponent.

Now it was the dwarf's turn. He carefully selected a stone and aimed at the target. With a precise movement, he threw the stone, and it hit the middle of the target with a powerful bang.

Round after round unfolded, and the competition became intense. Skrymir and the dwarf challenged each other with their best throws, pushing many of each other's stones away. There were moments of triumph and moments of frustration, but the atmosphere was filled with excitement and energy.

Skrymir seemed to lose all his gold if he couldn't remove the dwarf's stone from the target. He had picked up a large stone and was about to throw. With a bang, the door to the inn burst open. A dwarf shouted. "Odder is dead," "Odder is dead," "Come to the king's hall, Odder has been killed."

With that, the inn was emptied of dwarves, and everyone ran to the king's hall.

Skrymir ran along and stood at the back of the large hall. However, he was a lot taller than all the dwarves, so he could see most of it. There were shouts and screams from the dwarves. Skrymir, who had now had a lot of mead, couldn't really understand what was happening, and stood at the back admiring the throne room.

King Reidmar's throne room in Nidavellir is nothing less than a wonderful symphony of the dwarves' craftsmanship. Larger than even the most impressive halls in Asgard, it stretches like a labyrinth of shiny corridors and magnificent halls, flanked by columns and arches adorned with gemstones and precious metals.

In the middle of the throne room stood the throne, carved from the purest gold and inlaid with gemstones that glimmered like stars on a clear night. Along the walls hung treasures and trophies, collected from countless excavations and adventures, each with its own story and legend.

It is a place of unimaginable beauty and splendor, but also of deep respect and awe, for Reidmar's throne room is the heart of the dwarves' realm, and it is here where decisions are made and justice is administered. With a bang, he was awakened from his trance. Reidmar, who stood in front of the throne, slammed his axe into the ground, and then there was silence.

Reidmar, his voice filled with a mix of sorrow and anger that echoed through the impressive throne room.

"Brothers and sisters," he began, his voice filled with authority, "Today we stand united in sorrow." Our son Odder, one of our dearest, has been taken from us in the most cruel way"
"We have just been informed by Mimer, he saw that the god Loki has killed Odder"

A mumbling astonishment went through the assembly, and Reidmar continued with firmness in his voice: "But it must not go unpunished. "We must demand justice for Odder's death, and Loki must pay the price for his misdeeds."

His words were met with nods and agreement from the dwarves, and Reidmar raised his hand in a gesture of determination. "Let us gather our forces and prepare for battle." "We will not rest until Loki stands trial and pays for his actions."

With that, Reidmar raised his hammer, and the dwarves broke out in a powerful tribute to their leader and in memory of Odder, their fallen brother.

He pointed his hammer down towards a spot in the crowd of dwarves.

"Regin, my son, will you make a weapon worthy of a battle against Asgard," the king shouted.

Regin shouted back: "Yes, my king, I will make a weapon that will avenge my brother and make the gods tremble with fear."

Reidmar then pointed towards another place in the crowd of gathered dwarves and shouted.

"Ivaldi's sons, will you three make a weapon worthy of a battle against Asgard?"

The three Ivaldi Sons shouted in chorus: "Yes, our king, we will make a weapon that will give Odin nightmares."

Then Reidmar pointed down towards the place where Skrymir was standing, who was shocked when all the dwarves looked over at him.

"Sindri and Brokkr, will you make a weapon that can overcome Asgard?" the king shouted.

Skrymir looked at Sindri, who filled his lungs and straightened his back, and with a determined look shouted through the hall.

"We have long wanted to make a weapon better than Mjolner, and we will make a weapon that will make Mjolner look like a toy."

Reidmar then raised his axe: "Brothers and sisters, for a long time we have been looked down upon by the gods, for a long time they

Chapter 15: Odin

The door to the throne room creaked loudly as it opened, and in stepped Loki, Odin, and Høner. Their presence sent a wave of surprise through the assembly, and the dwarves gaped at the unexpected guests.

Skrymir, positioned at the back of the hall, watched the entrance of the three divine figures with a mix of awe and skepticism. His gaze first landed on Odin, the mighty All-Father, whose figure radiated an aura of wisdom and authority. Odin stood tall, his wise eyes seeming to peer into the souls of anyone who met his gaze. His long gray beard flowed like a river over his chest, and his one-eyed face was adorned with a wise smile, hinting at a deep understanding of the universe's secrets.

Beside Odin stood Høner, a smaller figure than the All-Father, but still radiating a certain vitality and cunning that could not be underestimated. Høner was dressed in simple garments, yet his eyes sparkled with sharp intelligence, matching Odin's. His gaze was always alert, as if waiting for the right moment to act.

Loki's arrival brought a wave of confusion and unrest. His figure was slim and agile, his features sharp and smooth as a serpent's. A sly glint danced in his green eyes, and a smile played on his lips, suggesting a type of cleverness few could resist. Loki carried his own aura of mystery and unpredictability, making him both fascinating and dangerous at the same time.

Skrymir observed the three divine figures with a mix of respect and caution, his mind filled with excitement about what would unfold next.

Reidmar's sharp gaze fixed on Loki, his face tightened with anger and grief. "What is the meaning of this unexpected visit, Loki?" he asked, his voice filled with cool authority.

Loki stepped forward with undisturbed confidence, his smile crooked and his gaze filled with hidden intentions. "I come with an offer," he said, his voice filled with a disturbing calm. "A deal that could benefit both us and you if you are willing to listen."

The dwarves around Reidmar exchanged nervous glances, hesitating between mistrust and curiosity. Odin, standing by Loki's side, observed the assembly with a calm and wise look, while Høner positioned himself as if they had some involvement in the upcoming conversation.

Reidmar clenched his teeth and stepped forward, his eyes still locked on Loki. "Let's hear what you have to say, Loki," he said, his voice a mix of distrust and curiosity. "But be warned, we will not accept deceit or treachery."

Loki smiled crookedly and nodded understandingly. "I assure you, Reidmar, this offer will benefit us both," he said, and proceeded to lay out his plan to the dwarves, who listened with a mix of skeptical interest and cautious hope.

Loki stood stiffly, his face expressing surprise at the accusation. "I swear by Asgard, Reidmar, I had no intention of killing Odder," he said, placing a hand on his chest as a sign of honesty. "I truly thought he was a regular otter, and I needed his skin as part of a deal."

Reidmar looked skeptical but seemed open to dialogue. "What do you propose then, Loki?" he asked, his voice tight yet open for negotiation.

Loki thought quickly, his mind working overtime to find a solution that would satisfy Reidmar while preserving his own reputation. "I will compensate you amply for your loss," he said, raising a hand to show his honesty. "I will bring you a treasure the likes of which you've never seen before." "Gold, silver, gemstones – everything your heart could desire."

Reidmar's face softened slightly at the thought of the potential treasure, but his mistrust was still evident. "And how can I trust that you will fulfill your part of the deal, Loki?" he asked, his voice filled with deep doubt.

Loki let a smile slip onto his lips, his gaze locked on Reidmar. "You can trust me, Reidmar," he assured, his voice filled with a conviction that almost sounded genuine. "I will personally ensure that you receive your treasure, and I will do whatever it takes to make amends."

Reidmar still looked skeptical, but there was a spark of hope in his eyes. "I will consider your offer, Loki," he said, turning to the dwarves around him. "But I expect the treasure to be of a size that matches my loss." "Nothing less will be accepted."

Loki nodded understandingly, his smile widening as he saw an opportunity to regain Reidmar's trust. "It will be as you wish, Reidmar," he said, his voice filled with a tone of expectation. "I will not disappoint you."

Loki, with his cunning eyes and fleeting smile, nodded briefly to Odin and Høner before turning on his heel and leaving the throne room. His steps were light and quick, as if he already had plans for how he would accomplish his task.

Behind him, Skrymir, still standing in the shadows, watched as Odin and Høner were detained by Reidmar's mighty dwarf warriors. The two divine beings did not resist, but it was clear they were not free to leave the hall. Their gazes followed Loki's departure, and their mere presence alone was enough to spread an aura of tension and anticipation in the air.

Skrymir could only imagine what magical and dangerous powers Loki would employ to bring the treasure back to Reidmar. If anyone could do it, it was the cunning and unpredictable Loki.

Meanwhile, Fenris and Alvis walked quietly, their minds heavy. Did Odder survive? Had the figure saved him? Fenris thought to himself.

"Let's go to Andvare, maybe he knows something," said Alvis.

"Okay," said Fenris sadly and began to walk slowly towards the river with Alvis on his back.

Andvare sat by the edge of the clear lake, staring into the water with a blank expression in his eyes. When he heard Fenris and Alvis approaching, he slowly turned his head towards them and asked in a faint voice, "What brings you here to me?"

Fenris and Alvis exchanged a worried glance before Alvis gathered the courage and said, "We have sad news to tell you, Andvare." "It's about your friend Odder, we believe he is dead."

Andvare stared in horror at them and slowly sank to his knees by the edge of the lake. Tears began to roll down his cheeks, and he whispered, "How could this happen?" "Who has done this to my friend?"

Alvis placed a comforting paw on his shoulder and replied, "It was an evil and dark figure, which none of us could have foreseen coming, but we will get revenge."

Loki, with his sly smile and a glint of triumph in his eye, stepped forward from the shadows. His presence filled the place with an inexplicable tension.

Fenris and Alvis exchanged a meaningful glance, "It's him, it's the figure," exclaimed Alvis.

Andvare looked at the figure, "I know who it is, it's Loki" "What have you done with Odder?" he shouted at Loki.

"Odder is fine!," said Loki with a voice that carried promises of betrayal and deceit. "He's swimming around down in Hellheim, where he belongs, and if you don't show me where your treasure is, you'll come down to him!" Meanwhile, Loki reached out for Andvare.

His words hung in the air like a threat, and Alvis looked at Fenris with despair in his eyes.

Andvare, whose heart pounded with fear and anger, knew he could not overcome Loki in sheer power. He had to use his cunning, the same cunning that had saved him from countless dangers before. With a quick glance at his friends, who nodded encouragingly, he gathered his will and transformed into a salmon. His sleek, silver-colored body slipped easily out of Loki's grasp and into the cold, clear water.

Loki, surprised and furious at this sudden deception, leaped after him, but Andvare was already far ahead. With powerful thrusts of his tail, he shot through the water, diving deep where he knew he could hide among rocks and water plants.

Fenris and Alvis, now left alone on the bank, looked worriedly at each other. "We must find a way to stop Loki before he catches Andvare," said Fenris with a grim tone. "And we must protect the treasure."

"Yes," replied Alvis, "But how? he is a god"

Meanwhile, Andvare swam desperately through the river's network, his mind racing with plans on how to secure his treasure and save the others from Loki's clutches. He knew he couldn't evade the god forever. Who could be strong enough to challenge Loki, could the serpent he had heard about, the one that keeps growing, be strong enough to challenge Loki. "Where can one find the serpent ?"

Suddenly he heard a shout through the water, it was Loki shouting. "Come up, or I'll kill the wolf and the beaver" Andvare stopped abruptly in his swimming, his heart pounding in his chest. Loki's threat echoed in his ears, and he knew he had no choice but to return. With heavy, reluctant movements, he swam back towards the sound of Loki's voice.

When he reached the riverbank, he saw the frightening sight. Fenris the wolf lay unconscious on the ground, surrounded by dark shadows, while Loki stood with a victorious smile, holding the beaver in an iron grip. Andvare's heart sank. He knew he was facing an almost impossible situation.

"Loki!" shouted Andvare, his voice filled with both fear and anger. "What do you want? Why are you doing this to me?"

Loki slowly turned towards Andvare, his eyes glinting with malice. "Ah, Andvare, finally you have come." You know what I want. Your treasure, and the legendary ring that can create wealth without end. Surrender it to me, and maybe... maybe I will spare your friends."

Andvare felt torn. The ring was not only a source of material wealth but also a family heirloom, tied to countless memories and powers. But what was a ring against the lives of those he cared about? In a moment of clarity, Andvare knew what he had to do.

"Take it," said Andvare, as he slowly approached Loki and pulled the gleaming ring from his neck. "But you must promise me that you will let Fenris and Alvis go free." "Then you may have my treasure."

With a crooked smile and with the ring in hand, Loki said, "So be it, but many will regret this." He pulled out a net, which he used to tie up Andvare, Fenris, and Alvis.

Before Loki got the location of the treasure, he told them that the net was a gift from Ran, which could be used to catch Andvare, but thanks to the wolf and the beaver, it didn't even need to be used.

Andvare told where he could find his treasure, and away went Loki. Now the three lay, bound by Ran's net. Fenris slowly woke up and came to himself.

"What happened?" he asked.

"Loki has stolen my treasure, and my precious ring," Andvare told him "Why would he want that?" Asked Fenris "What does a god need with a treasure?"

Andvare looked thoughtful. "It must be Ran behind it, Loki told me he had received the net from her", "She must be out to get the greatest treasure in Jotunheim"

"That makes sense!" Said Fenris, opened his mouth and bit a large chunk of the net. "Such a small net, might hold a fish, but not a wolf" he laughed.

"This will Ran regret!" said Andvare loudly. "Help me gather the gold he didn't take", "we must summon the Norns", "we must go to Mimir's well" Follow me.

They went to Mimir's well, and saw Mimir, who was examining the bite marks that were in his tree. He tried to cover them up so that no disease would get into the tree.

Meanwhile, they could sneak up to the well, where they could summon the Norns.

Andvare stared down into the well and said: "Norns, I call you to me, for my friend has been killed." Come and see the treasure I have brought to you, as payment for a little help."

A puff sounded, and suddenly there stood three old, white-clad women with scissors in their hands.

"Welcome, Urd, Verdandi, and Skuld," said Andvare.

"How have you convinced Mimir to allow you to use his well?" "You are neither king nor god," said Urd with a hoarse, old voice.

"Mimir knows my sorrows and has given me permission to request your help," Andvare replied.

"Remember, dwarf, that we control past, present, and future, so you cannot lie to us. "Tell us what you want with us, we can't stand here all day, ends with Yggdrasil withering away" said Urd.

"I have brought a treasure with me to you, the finest treasure with the rarest gemstones," said Andvare.

"You could have just said that, dwarf. What can we help you with?" asked Urd as they began to examine the treasure.

"Ran, in league with Loki, has stolen my ring and part of my treasure and killed my friend. I want the ring and the treasure to be cursed, so Ran can feel the pain I feel."

Urd looked away from the treasure and towards Andvare. "We must not manipulate the timeline, but it is a fine treasure you have," she said.

"What do you want to happen to the owner of the treasure?" Asked Skuld

Fenris whispered to Andvare, "Ran sent a big dragon at us, maybe one could…"

Andvare grinned slyly, "the owner of the ring shall become a dragon"

"Change the life thread, so one becomes a dragon?" "Don't even know if we have any dragon life thread" "What do you say ladies?" " asked Urd and looked at Verdandi and Skuld, who were trying on necklaces.

Skuld said with the necklace around her neck, "it will be difficult, but see how pretty this one is on me." "If only dwarves could see their life thread" whispered Verdande. "Let's go home". Puff, then they were gone.

"Can't wait to see Ran as a dragon", Andvare laughed to himself. "Would you like to come down and visit Ran?" he asked the others.

"I would like to," said Alvis.

"I must go to Skrymir, and see what he is doing" said Fenris.

They said goodbye, and then Fenris began to walk towards the dwarf world, where Skrymir still was.

Meanwhile, Loki, with the treasure and ring safely in his possession, returned to Reidmar's mighty hall. His return was marked by a triumphant atmosphere, knowing that he had achieved what many had considered impossible. Reidmar, the greedy dwarf king, received him with a mix of admiration and envy.

When he arrived at the hall, where Odin and Høner were still being held, he presented the treasure to Reidmar. The dwarf king's eyes lit up at the sight of the legendary ring and the other valuable items, now lying at his feet.

"You've done it, Loki," said Reidmar with a voice shaking with greed and satisfaction. "You have secured our wealth and power for generations to come."

With a broad smile and a gesture of power, Reidmar commanded his warriors to release Odin and Høner. The two divine beings rose, their faces expressionless, but their eyes burned with a calm, but intense anger.

"You have played your game well, Loki," said Odin calmly, as he fixed his gaze on Reidmar. "But be careful, for the game is far from over."

Loki nodded, well aware that his actions had created new alliances and enemies.
He left the hall with a crooked smile, while Odin and Høner slowly left the dwarf domain, their thoughts already focused on future plans and reprisals.
Before leaving the hall, Loki turned around with a crooked smile, "King Reidmar, take care of the treasure, hide it deep in Nidavellir", "Can sense fire, and destruction in that treasure"

Reidmar waved him away, while he looked captivatingly at the treasure.

Reidmar motioned to one of his guards, "Summon my sons".

It wasn't long before Regin and Fafner stood before him in the throne room.

"Sons, see how mighty and rich your father has become... We have become", "Because you are my sons, you may each choose one thing from the treasure"

"Just one thing?" Exclaimed Fafner, "But there is so much, can't possibly just choose one thing"

Regin walked towards the treasure, and was about to take Andvare's ring, just as he was about to take it, Fafner snatched the ring in front of him.

"It fits better on me" Exclaimed Fafner with a sly grin

Regin looked with an evil gaze at his brother Fafner, who had always felt elevated above him.

"A good choice my son, a magic ring that can make gold", "It shall be called Andvaranaut, in memory of a dwarf, who once had a ring that looked like."

"Father, king, if I could just borrow Fafner's ring once in a while, I could make many weapons" "weapons of the finest gold, without having to buy gold", "The ring can make the gold for the weapons"

"Good idea, my dear son, we will be the mightiest world, soon Asgard will have to worship us" Exclaimed the king proudly

"No!, shouted Fafner, "the ring is mine!" He put the ring on, and immediately one could see a glow in his eyes. He turned around, and then he was gone.

"He will be good again", said the king "What a day it has been", let's go to bed, from tomorrow weapons will be made.

"Looking forward to seeing Odin's face, when he faces an army of dwarves with weapons of gold." Reidmar laughed, as he walked towards his bedroom. "Bring the treasure to my chamber, will sleep on gold tonight"

It was now early the next morning, one could hear a snoring go through Nidavellir and occasional hammering of iron against iron.

Fenris had finally found Skrymir, who was sleeping in a large pile of hay. He licked him on the cheek, and Skrymir woke up with a start.

"Fenris!" "Good to see you my friend!" Said Skrymir with a smile "Did you find Andvare? How is he?"

Fenris sighed deeply, his eyes darker than the deepest part of an old forest. "Yes, I found Andvare, but Loki... he has stolen Andvare's gold." "Andvare has enchanted the treasure, so it brings misfortune over anyone who possesses it."

Skrymir sat up with a jerk, his face became

Chapter 16: The Dragon

They ran through Nidavellir and arrived at Reidmar's bedroom. They could smell a faint scent of burnt wood. They opened the door and saw that the bedroom had been ransacked. In the corner lay Reidmar in a dire state. There were scratch marks on furniture and walls, and still fire that had not yet been extinguished.

Fenris and Skrymir stood next to the dying Reidmar, whose breathing was weak and uneven. The fire from the burning hut cast flickering shadows over his tired face. Meanwhile, guards had entered, searching the bedroom for clues as to who had harmed the king.

"The treasure is gone, stolen," Reidmar whispered with a voice as weak as a breeze.

"Tell us what the culprit looked like, king, and we shall avenge you, we will gather all of Nidavellir and avenge you," exclaimed one of the guards.

"No, no dwarf may harm the one who stole the treasure." Reidmar coughed, "Summon Beowulf," He will be able to find the treasure.

Skrymir clenched his fists in frustration. "Loki... he is the root of all this evil. He brought the cursed treasure..."

Meanwhile, Reidmar's son Regin entered and threw himself down to his dying father. "Who has done this?"

"The treasure is cursed," Fenris explained. "Andvari cast a curse over the treasure, so it would bring misfortune and destruction to anyone who possessed it, without knowing its true nature. Loki knew this, but it did not stop him. Reidmar only saw the shine of the gold, not the darkness that came with it."

Skrymir shook his head in disbelief. "So what do we do now?" "How do we stop this destruction?"

"Summon Beowulf," Regin firmly told one of the guards. "He is among the few who can retrieve the treasure."

Not long after, Beowulf entered the king's chamber with an aura of calm and determination. He was a large man, broad-shouldered and muscular, dressed in worn leather armor that bore the marks of many previous battles. His hair was light and closely cropped, and his eyes had a sharp, penetrating blue color that reflected a lifelong dedication to combating evil and injustice. By his side was Sigurd, younger and with a fiery energy that contrasted Beowulf's more measured approach. Sigurd was lean but strongly built, with dark, shoulder-length hair and intense searching eyes. His armor was less worn, shiny and well-maintained, indicating his status as a rising star among warriors.

Beowulf, with his broad shoulders and sharp eyes, listened attentively to Fenris's account of the cursed treasure. Sigurd nodded understandingly.

"Good, we need you to help find the one who stole the treasure."
"Will you help Skrymir and Fenris?" said Beowulf

"Yes," replied Skrymir, "The treasure is too dangerous, it must be kept in a safe place" Fenris nodded.

"We are facing a great challenge," said Beowulf, his voice filled with a calm authority. "Whoever has stolen the treasure is transformed by the treasure's power and curse." "It will take more than steel to defeat it and break the curse."

Regin declared with a firm voice, "Sigurd, follow me. I will forge you a sword, worthy of avenging my father." Without hesitation, Sigurd followed Regin.

"Good, prepare yourselves, for when Sigurd returns, we set out and find out who stole the treasure." Said Beowulf firmly,

"I wish to speak with Beowulf privately," declared the king. "Everyone else, leave the chamber now!" Fenris and Skrymir left the bedroom with the guards.

Shortly after, Beowulf stepped out of the chamber, his eyes slightly heavy with fatigue. He looked with a vacant gaze, his steps laden with concern.

Without saying a word, he cast a glance at Fenris and Skrymir and signaled that they should follow him to Regin's workshop. Together they set off in silence, while the sound of hammers striking anvils filled the air around them. Skrymir and Fenris followed closely behind him, their faces a mix of hope and anxiety.

When they reached the forge, they could see Regin in full swing. Sparks flew around him like stars in the night sky as he worked on the new sword. Sigurd stood by his side, his face serious and focused on the work being performed.

"Regin, how is the sword coming along?" asked Beowulf, his voice cutting through the sound of the metal.

Regin paused and looked up with a proud smile. "Ah, Beowulf, you come at just the right time. I have just completed the sword. Look here," he said, lifting the finished weapon from the anvil. The sword, which he had named Gram, shone with an almost supernatural sheen, its blade engraved with ancient runes and symbols.

Sigurd stepped forward and carefully took the sword in his hands. He lifted it, examined it in the light, and the sword seemed to sing with a quiet but powerful tone. "It's beautiful," he said, his voice filled with awe.

"It's more than beautiful, it's powerful," added Regin. "Gram is forged from the strongest steel and blessed by the ancient gods. It is the only sword that can break the curse that rests on the stolen treasure."

Beowulf nodded appreciatively. "Then we are ready. With Gram by our side, we shall find the thief and bring the treasure back where it belongs."

Skrymir gave Sigurd a strong pat on the shoulder. "We need all the help we can gather. With this dark magic loose, we cannot know what awaits us."

Fenris, who had been silent until now, stepped forward. "Let's not waste more time. The longer we wait, the stronger the curse becomes."

With a newfound determination in their hearts, the group prepared to leave the forge. They knew that the journey they were facing would be filled with dangers, but with Gram by their side, they felt ready to face anything.

After many hours of exhausting trek through narrow, winding

passages in the underground tunnels, which twisted like labyrinths under the ground, they finally reached a large cave. Here, the light from their flickering torches cast long, dancing shadows on the rough walls. The air was damp and heavy, and every sound seemed to be amplified in the enormous cavity.

Suddenly, a deep, grunting sound filled the cave, and it echoed eerily between the stone formations. With hearts pounding, they tightened their grip on their weapons, felt the weight and coldness of the metal, and moved cautiously forward, while sharp eyes scouted the darkness ahead.

In front of them, in the vast, dimly lit cave, a colossal dragon appeared. Its massive body was covered in shiny scales, which sparkled like thousands of tiny diamonds under the flickering glow from the surrounding torches. The mighty wings were carefully folded along its back, and each breath caused them to gently wave. The dragon's eyes, deep and glowing like molten lava, locked onto them with an intensity that could freeze the blood in their veins. From the powerful jaws, filled with rows of sharp, serrated teeth, thin streams of smoke seeped, while a heavy, burning breath escaped and filled the air with a sulfuric stench.

With a voice so deep and resonant that it made the stone-paved walls of the cave vibrate, the dragon roared, "Who dares to trespass in my domain?" Each word rolled through the room like thunder, and the echo slowly died away between the sharp stalactites that hung from the ceiling like inverted spears.

Sigurd stepped forward with decisive steps, his steel-gray eyes fixed on the mighty dragon. With a firm grip, he lifted the sword Gram, which glinted menacingly in the dim light from the flickering torches set up around the cave. "We have not come here to fight," he said with a voice that echoed against the damp cave walls. "We seek a stolen treasure that rightfully belongs to the dwarves. Give us the treasure, and we will leave your domain without further strife."

The dragon, whose scales glinted like a thousand tiny mirrors in the light, snorted contemptuously, and thick, gray smoke began to seep out between its tightly clenched teeth. Its eyes, glowing like coal, fixed hard on Sigurd and his companions. "The treasure is mine!" roared the dragon with a voice that made the cave shake.

At this point, Beowulf stepped forward, his figure calm but determined, as he approached the dragon. "The treasure you guard bears a heavy curse," he said, dodging a stream of warm breath from the dragon. "It brings misfortune over anyone who possesses it. Let us not fight, but instead seek a way to break this curse.."

The dragon's massive head tilted slightly, as if considering Beowulf's words. Around them, the cave buzzed with tension and uncertainty, while they awaited the dragon's next move.

The dragon stared at them with its deep, glowing eyes, lighting up the dim cave. Each breath it took sent small clouds of smoke out between its sharp teeth. "No one," hissed the dragon with a voice that sounded like crushing stone, "shall steal my treasure." Beowulf took a step closer, his voice firm and resolute. "If it is battle you wish, then let it be so." He looked over at Sigurd, Fenris, and Skrymir, and nodded briefly to them. They positioned themselves by his side, ready for battle.

The dragon, now understanding that these intruders would not back down without a fight, rose up on its hind legs and let out a roar that made the cave vibrate. Flames began to form deep inside its throat.

Sigurd was the first to react. With a powerful swing, he sent Gram swinging through the air, a beam of blue light following the sword as it cut through the thick smoke. The dragon dodged with a quick movement of its head, but was still hit on one of its massive scales, leaving a glowing red mark.

Fenris, smaller in size but quick on his feet, ran forward and jumped up, grabbing one of the dragon's wings with his claws. He used his weight to pull the wing downward, bringing the dragon off balance.

Skrymir, grabbed a large stone from the floor and threw it towards the dragon's head. The stone hit with a loud bang, and the dragon shook its head angrily, clearly affected.

Beowulf, having waited for the right moment, took a powerful run-up and jumped towards the dragon's chest, where he struck one of the smaller scales with his huge battle axe. The axe cut deeply, and the dragon let out a painful roar.

The dragon, now furious and clearly affected by the pain, swung its massive tail with such violent force that the ground shook beneath them. All four warriors were thrown back, their armor clanging against the sharp stones on the cave floor. Mists of smoke and intense flames filled the dim room, and the heat from the dragon's preparation to spew a stream of fire felt almost unbearable.

The dragon opened its gigantic mouth to release its flaming breath, shouted Beowulf with a voice that cut through the noise, "Now!" At his signal, all four warriors threw themselves to each side at the last moment. The flames licked just past them, leaving traces of scorched earth and stone.

The four warriors quickly regrouped, their gazes locked on the dragon, which now seemed a bit confused by their quick maneuvers. They knew this was their chance. With a renewed, collective strength, they charged towards the colossal beast.

Sigurd and Beowulf, armed with flashing swords, attacked the dragon from the front, their weapons creating sparks as they hit the dragon's shiny scales. On the flanks, Fenris and Skrymir moved quickly and silently, their axes swinging in wide, deadly arcs. The dragon, now clearly overwhelmed by their coordinated and relentless attack, began to wobble and lose its strength. Each strike from the warriors' weapons made it roar in pain and frustration.After an intense battle, where the dragon had tried to fend off the warriors' attacks with its mighty wings and fire-breathing breath, its powers began to wane. Sigurd and Beowulf pressed on with renewed energy, their swords dancing in the air, each hit sending shockwaves through the dragon's armor. Fenris and Skrymir, now also sensing the proximity of victory, carefully surrounded the dragon from the sides, avoiding the desperate swings from its tail.

The dragon, surrounded and exhausted, tried one last time to rise and spray a whirl of flames at its attackers. But this time, its fire was weaker, and the warriors' shields and armor held firm. With a collective effort and a shout that could be heard across the entire battlefield, the warriors gathered their forces and charged together against the dragon.

Sigurd leaped forward and thrust his sword deep into a weak spot under the dragon's wing, while Beowulf struck another vital area near the neck. Overwhelmed by pain and exhaustion, the dragon collapsed, its eyes losing their fire, and its breath growing weaker.

Just as Sigurd raised his sword to deliver a perhaps fatal blow, Beowulf stepped forward with firm steps, his eyes burning with a mix of determination and seriousness. "Sigurd, wait," he said with a voice that bore traces of both respect and a certain immobility. "We cannot kill the dragon. We must find a way to lift the curse."

Sigurd hesitated, torn between his duty as a warrior and his comrade's words. The dragon, sensing the shift in the air, looked at them with lost eyes.

Sigurd lowered his sword.

The dragon looked confused at Sigurd, who lowered his sword. A moment of silence hung in the air before the dragon suddenly let out a furious roar and snapped at Beowulf. Its scaly jaws closed around Beowulf, who was pierced by the sharp teeth.

Beowulf roared in pain, but his face did not contort in fear. Instead, he looked deeply into the dragon's eyes and said with a firm voice: "We can save you, we can break the curse, but you must let us help you." Meanwhile, Sigurd raised his sword towards the sky, the light glinting on the sharp steel. With a powerful swing, he cut through the air and struck the dragon right in its scaly chest. A loud roar filled the air, the dragon released Beowulf and staggered backwards before falling to the ground with a thud.

Beowulf, struggling with the pain from the dragon's bite, looked astonished at Sigurd before collapsing on the ground.

They rushed to Beowulf, who lay pale and wounded on the ground. Sigurd knelt by his side and grabbed his hand. "Hang in there, Beowulf." "We will save you," he said with tears in his eyes.

Meanwhile, the dragon slowly began to transform back into its former form. The scales disappeared, and instead, a dwarf with gray hair and tired eyes appeared.

Beowulf looked up in surprise at the transformed dragon and smiled faintly. "You are free, Fafner," he said quietly. Fafner nodded gratefully. "Thank you, brave warriors, for freeing me from this curse," he said before his eyes dimmed.

Beowulf grabbed Sigurd's hand and said with a weak voice: "Take care of our land, Sigurd. "Be a protector and a guard against evil." Sigurd promised and stood up with gram in hand.

Beowulf smiled one last time before closing his eyes. A quiet peace settled over the cave, and he bid farewell to his brave leader. In the twilight's subdued light, Fenris, the giant wolf, approached with heavy, purposeful steps. With a mix of caution and reverence, he gently lifted Fafner's lifeless, bloody body onto his broad back. His eyes, deep as the night's darkness, rested for a moment on Beowulf with an intensity that reflected both respect and a deep, smoldering sorrow. With careful movements, he also lifted Beowulf's fallen body and placed him next to Fafnir.

Sigurd, gathering the treasure that glittered despite the cave's dimness, into his arms. Each piece of gold and every gemstone was a reminder of Beowulf's last words and his unwavering promise to protect the land from all threats.

With Fafnir and Beowulf resting on Fenris' back, and a treasure that symbolized more than wealth, Sigurd, Fenris, and Skrymir left the dark cave.

When they reached the king's hall, Regin was there to receive them. His face was marked by a heavy mix of awe and sorrow over the loss of a brother.

Sigurd stood before Regin in the king's hall, his voice filled with awe and sorrow. He told of Beowulf's invincible courage, of how he stood firm against Fafner who had been transformed into a dragon so fearsome and malevolent that even the mountains shook with fear.

He described Beowulf's final battle, his heroic fight against Fafner, where he fought with a strength and courage that were unparalleled. Sigurd described how Beowulf fell in battle, but not before he had deeply wounded the dragon and freed Fafner from the spell.

Regin listened intently to Sigurd's words, his face expressing sorrow. He thanked Sigurd for bringing Fafner's body back and honoring his memory in this way.

The king rose slowly from his throne, a dwarf whose age and wisdom were engraved in the deep lines of his face. His eyes, which had seen many years and many battles, were moist with sorrow over the loss of Fafner.

With dignified steps, he approached Regin and Sigurd, who stood next to the large, covered form that was Fafner's body. The king placed a hand on him, his touch almost sacred, and for a moment, time stood still in the heavy air of the king's hall.

With the help of his closest dwarf warriors, the king carefully lifted Fafner's body. They carried him with a respectful calm, as if they were aware of the honor it was to handle a fallen hero. They moved through the hall, where dwarves stood in silent awe, some with their heads bowed in a final tribute.

They left the hall through the large double doors, which opened with a creak, as if even the castle's old stones felt the weight of the moment. Outside, a procession awaited, ready to lead Fafner to his final resting place. A gentle breeze carried the scent of pine and earth, a reminder of life's continued course despite everything.

Regin, with a serious expression in his eyes, turned to Sigurd and said in a deep voice: "Sigurd, you have performed a service of invaluable worth for our kingdom and our people. Now it is crucial that you bring the treasure to my workshop, so I can lift its dark curse and ensure that its evil power no longer casts shadows over us."

Sigurd nodded understandingly and followed Regin through winding paths to the hidden workshop, where he carefully handed over the treasure.

After delivering the treasure, Sigurd met with Skrymir and Fenris at an old, cozy inn. They sat at a sturdy oak table, and soon the air smelled of honey and malt as they toasted in golden mead. They talked about their recent battle against the dragon

Printed in Great Britain
by Amazon